WHEN THE SNOW FELL

READ MORE ABOUT
JOEL GUSTAFSON'S ADVENTURES
IN THESE COMPANION NOVELS

A BRIDGE TO THE STARS
SHADOWS IN THE TWILIGHT

WHEN THE SNOW FELL

HENNING MANKELL

TRANSLATED FROM THE SWEDISH
BY LAURIE THOMPSON

DELACORTE PRESS

Translation copyright © 2007 by Laurie Thompson

All rights reserved. Published in the United States by Delacorte Press, an imprint of Random House Children's Books, a division of Random House, Inc., New York. Originally published in Sweden as *Pojken som sov med snö i sin säng* by Henning Mankell, copyright © 1996 by Henning Mankell, by Rabén & Sjögren, Stockholm, in 1996. This translation was originally published in Great Britain by Andersen Press, Limited, London, in 2007.

Delacorte Press is a registered trademark and the colophon is a trademark of Random House, Inc.

Visit us on the Web! www.randomhouse.com/teens

Library of Congress Cataloging-in-Publication Data

Mankell, Henning.
[Pojken som sov med snö i sin säng. English]
When the snow fell / Henning Mankell ; translated from the
Swedish by Laurie Thompson.
p. cm.
Summary: Now almost fourteen, Joel becomes a local hero to his small Swedish town when he saves an old man from freezing to death in the woods.
ISBN 978-0-385-73497-4 (alk. paper) — ISBN 978-0-385-90491-9 (lib. bdg.)
[1. Single-parent families—Fiction. 2. Fathers and sons—Fiction. 3. Sweden—History—20th century—Fiction.] I. Thompson, Laurie. II. Title.
PZ7.M31283Wh 2009
[Fic]—dc22
2008020623

The text of this book is set in 12-point Goudy.

Book design by Kenny Holcomb

Printed in the United States of America
10 9 8 7 6 5 4 3 2 1
First American Edition

WHEN THE SNOW FELL

JUST BEFORE THE SILENT SNOW BEGINS TO FALL . . .

Stories have been told about Joel before now. About him growing up in a little town in the north of Sweden. It's the 1950s. Such a long time ago. But it seems very recent even so.

He grows up in a house with walls that creak in the very cold winters. It's on the bank of a river with clean, clear water flowing to the sea he has never seen. He lives with his dad, Samuel, a lumberjack who doesn't say much. Samuel used to be a sailor, and still longs to get away from the gloomy forests and return to the sea, but he can never bring himself to move. They live together in that house, Joel Gustafson and his father. And both of them dream, in their different ways, about Joel's mum, Jenny, who simply vanished one day. Packed a suitcase and went away. She is out there somewhere, but she's gone, she's left Joel and his dad to look after each other. Nobody knows where she is.

The spruce forests are silent.

One night Joel sees a dog running through the cold winter darkness. Something has woken him up. He sits on a window seat, looks out and suddenly sees the dog. It's trotting on silent paws, heading for some unknown destination. Joel sees it for a couple of seconds, and then it's gone.

Joel can't forget that dog. Where was it heading? Where did it come from? *Where is Joel heading?* He forms a secret society to look for the dog. Or perhaps it's to find out who he himself really is. A secret society in which he is the only member. But the dog never returns. Joel never finds any tracks in the snow. It dawns on him in the end that the dog is heading for a distant, nameless star.

A dog on its way to somewhere beyond Orion. Heading for a constellation that maybe doesn't even exist. That only exists inside Joel's head.

The Winter of the Dog is a winter Joel will never forget. It's then that he begins to understand that he's himself, and nobody else. But he grows up, he grows older, he becomes thirteen. And he forgets about the dog. One day he's run over by a bus. He experiences a miracle. He falls between the wheels of the bus and is not injured at all. He discovers the hard way that a miracle can be very difficult to understand. But he learns. And everything else has suddenly become much more important than that solitary dog.

To grow up is to wonder about things; to be grown up is to slowly forget the things you wondered about as a child. He has realized this. And he doesn't want to become a grown-up like that.

He visits Gertrud, a young woman without a nose, more and more frequently. She lives alone in a strange house on the south side of the river, on the other side of the menacing railway bridge. He shares a lot of secrets with Gertrud. Lots of fun. But also sorrow and disappointment.

Time refuses to stand still.

It continues to run past.

And Joel runs alongside it. From his panting breath comes day after day, month after month. The snow melts, and up sprouts the new spring, when the ice thaws and breaks up on the big, wide river, and logs start to float past once more on their long journey to the sawmills by the sea. Then comes another summer, when the mosquitoes whine and the sun never seems to grow tired of shining. Then it's autumn, when the lingonberries ripen, when the leaves fall and the frost crackles under the rubber tires of his bicycle. Joel cycles a lot. He rides nonstop through the streets, searching for the unexpected.

Perhaps it will be round the next corner. Or the one after that. Or the one after that.

There comes an autumn when he is looking forward to his fourteenth birthday. Now he is fast asleep in his bed. Somewhere inside the wall, right next to his ear, a mouse is gnawing away. But he doesn't hear it. Nobody knows what he's dreaming about.

Outside, the silent snow starts to fall through the night.

There's a long time to go before dawn.

— ONE —

Joel let the roller blind run up very fast, so as to make a loud smacking noise.

It was like firing a cannon to salute the new day.

He stared out the window in surprise. The ground was all white. He had been fooled yet again.

Winter always came creeping up on you when you least expected it. Joel had decided last autumn that he would never allow that to happen again. Before going to bed, he would make up his mind whether or not it would start snowing during the night.

The problem was that you couldn't hear it snowing. It was different with rain. Rain pattered onto the corrugated iron roof over the cycle rack outside the front door. When the sun shone you couldn't hear that either, but the light changed. Wind was easiest of all.

5

Sometimes when it was blowing really hard, it would whip into the walls so fiercely that it felt as if the house was about to take off.

But snow came creeping up on you. Snow was like an Indian. It moved silently and came when you least expected it.

Joel continued gazing out the window. So winter had arrived now. There was no getting away from it. And he'd been fooled again. Would it be a long, cold winter? The snow that had fallen now would stay the longest. Because it would be underneath all the snow that came later. The first to come was the last to thaw. And that would be at the end of April, or even the beginning of May.

By then Joel would be fourteen. He'd have grown almost half an inch. And lots of things that he knew nothing about now would have happened.

The snow had arrived.

And so it was New Year's Eve. Even if it was still only November.

That was how it was for Joel. He had decided. New Year's Eve would be when the first snow fell.

His very own New Year's Eve. When the ground was white, that was when he would make his New Year's resolutions. If he had any.

And he did. Lots.

It was cold on the floor. Joel fetched a pillow from his bed and put it under his feet. He could hear his dad clattering about in the kitchen with the coffeepot. Samuel didn't like Joel standing on his pillow, so he would have to be ready to move away smartly from the window if the door suddenly opened behind him. But Samuel rarely came into Joel's bedroom in the morning. There was a risk, but not much of one.

He watched a single snowflake slowly floating down to the ground, to be swallowed up by all the whiteness.

There was a lot to think about when you were thirteen years of age. More than when you were twelve. Not to mention when you were eleven.

He thought he had learnt two things since it had started snowing last autumn: Life became more complicated as time passed by. And winter always came creeping up on you when you least expected it.

Joel thought about the previous evening. It had still been autumn then. After dinner he had pulled on his boots, grabbed hold of his jacket and leapt downstairs in three jumps. As it was a Sunday evening, the night train heading south stopped at the local railway station. It was rare for anybody to go aboard. And even rarer for anybody to get off. But you never knew. Besides, Joel used to slip little secret letters into the postbox in the mail coach.

I have my eye on you. Signed *J*.

Always the same text. But he would write different names on the envelope, taken at random from his dad's newspaper. He made up the addresses himself.

9 Miracle Street. Or *12 Blacksmith Lundberg's Avenue.*

Joel thought that there might be an address like that somewhere in the world. But as he also suspected that the post office had secret employees who spent all day and night tracing people who sent letters to invented addresses, he didn't dare to use the names of towns that really existed. And so he would study the latest issue of *Where When How* in the school library. That was an annual that listed things that had happened the previous year. Right at the back was a list of all the towns and villages in Sweden. It told you which places had grown bigger and which ones had become smaller. The little town where Joel lived always grew smaller every year. That confirmed Joel's suspicions. Nobody wanted to carry on living here. Nor did anybody want to move here. If things turned out really badly, he and Samuel would be the last two people in the place. He'd once tried to explain this to Samuel, but his dad only laughed.

"There'll always be people living by the river," he'd said.

"But does it have to be us?" Joel had asked.

Samuel didn't respond to that. He just laughed again, put on his glasses and started reading his newspaper. But Joel had been able to check in *Where When How* that the towns he had written on his envelopes did not exist in Sweden. Neither *Joelsville* nor *Sprucehampton*.

He never stuck stamps on the envelopes. He drew them on instead. Old men with long noses. As the letters were fakes, he didn't think it was right to use genuine postage stamps. And then he had to be careful when he slipped them into the postbox on the mail coach. Stationmaster Knif had sharp eyes, and was apt to flare up and lose his temper. But Joel hadn't been found out so far. He'd written in his notebook that he had now sent eleven letters in all with the southbound express train.

Anyway, he'd posted his latest letter the previous night. When it was still only autumn. The frost had crackled under his bicycle tires. Steam had billowed out from his mouth as he rode up the hill to the station and became short of breath. It was the middle of November. It had often started snowing by then, but not this year. Winter was late. But now, yet again, the snow had come creeping up during the night.

Joel glanced at the alarm clock on a stool next to his bed. He had better get a move on if he was going to be in time for school. He was behind schedule already, as usual. He shuffled into the bathroom, got washed as quickly as possible, dressed and went to the kitchen.

Samuel was getting ready to leave for work. His dad, the sailor who had become a lumberjack. Joel had often wished it was the other way round. The lumberjack who'd become a sailor. Then they wouldn't have lived here by the river, as far away from the sea as it was possible to get. Standing on a shelf was a model of an old sailing ship called *Celestine*. If things had been different, it would have been hanging on the wall of a cabin, being rocked by the gentle waves of the sea.

Joel sometimes thought about how impossible it was to understand grown-ups. They often had no idea what was best for them. They were always going on about how they wanted to do whatever they could to ensure that their children had a good life—but how could that be possible if they couldn't even look after themselves properly?

All those years, since Jenny had left, Joel had been his own mother. He'd never had any difficulty knowing what was best for himself. But Samuel was a hopeless case. He always said that *one day, soon, not just yet, but soon* they would pack up and leave. But it never happened. And Joel had started to despair long ago.

Samuel was just like all other adults. He had no idea what was best for him. And now he was too old. Too old to learn, and too old to allow Joel to make the decisions.

Samuel finished his coffee and rinsed out his cup.

Now he's going to tell me that I must get a move on, Joel thought.

"You'd better get a move on, or you'll be late for school," Samuel said.

Joel was kneeling down in front of a cupboard that contained everything from shoes to old newspapers. He was looking for his winter boots.

He knew that Samuel would now ask him if he'd heard.

"Did you hear what I said?" Samuel asked.

"Yes," said Joel. "But I won't be late. I'll get there in time."

Joel sat down in order to put his boots on. He gave them a good shaking first: mouse pooh fell out onto the floor. But no dead mice. There had been one in his left boot the previous winter. In the meantime Samuel was packing his rucksack. Some sandwiches, a bottle of milk and a thermos flask of coffee. Joel eyed him without making it obvious.

His dad was old. Even though he was only forty-one. But his back wasn't as straight as it used to be. And his face was thinner.

In addition, he shaved less often, and more carelessly.

Joel didn't like this. It was as if a cold wind had blown right through him. He didn't want a dad with a hunched back and unshaven cheeks.

But he also thought about the New Year's resolutions he would make that evening. His own secret New Year's Eve that nobody else knew about.

It was something he'd been thinking about for ages. Evening after evening he'd gone cycling round the little town, without thinking of anything else.

He'd made up his mind that he was going to live until he was at least a hundred years old. That would mean that he'd live until the year 2045. It was such an incredibly long way away that it really meant he would live forever.

But Joel knew that if he was going to achieve that aim,

he would have to start preparing himself even now. If he didn't, he would end up with a back just as hunched as Samuel's.

That was really the most important thing. More important than living to be a hundred. He didn't want to have a hunched back.

He knew what he was going to do in order to ensure that. It was one of the New Year's resolutions he would make that evening.

From tomorrow onwards, he would start toughening himself up. He had a plan, and he would carry it out once winter had established itself.

He was quite sure about it.

If you wanted to become really old, you had to toughen yourself up.

His train of thought was broken because Samuel was ready to leave for work. He put on his thick wooly hat, then turned round in the doorway and looked at Joel. Samuel often looked sad when he set off for work. That was something Joel didn't like either. It could give him a stomachache. It was at moments like that when he found it impossible to understand what Samuel was thinking.

He might be thinking about Mummy Jenny, who had simply vanished all those years ago. That could make Samuel just as sad as Joel could be.

Or was he thinking about the sea, which he wasn't

going to get to see today either? Among all those pines and firs that he chopped down and trimmed?

"Don't just sit there dreaming," he said. "That will make you late for school."

"I'm setting off as soon as I've got my boots on," Joel said.

"It's winter again now," said Samuel with a sigh. "And you can bet your life that winter's going to be long, and dark, and cold."

"We could move away from here," said Joel. "Tomorrow."

"If only it was as easy as that," said Samuel. "But it isn't."

Then he left. Joel could hear his footsteps on the stairs. The front door closed with a bang.

Joel fastened his boots. Put on his jacket, wooly hat and scarf. He couldn't find his mittens. He would have to choose between looking for them, and arriving on time for school.

He chose to forget about his mittens. It wasn't all that cold yet. Winter had only just begun.

He also decided not to take his bike. It could be good to test his boots. Kick up a bit of thin, powdery snow. But even as he started walking downstairs he could feel that they were starting to be too small. He needed a new pair. But how would he be able to convince Samuel of that? Boots were expensive.

"Being poor is expensive," Samuel often said. Joel thought he almost understood what his dad meant.

He went out into the street. It was still dark. Only a narrow sliver of light oozed out over the spruce forests standing to attention around the little town.

School beckoned. Miss Nederström was bound to be there already. If he got a move on, he would arrive in time.

He kicked up a flurry of snow.

He was already thinking about the coming evening, when he would make his solemn New Year's resolutions.

Winter had fooled him this year yet again.

But that didn't really matter.

The important thing was that a new year had begun.

— TWO —

On the way home from school Joel bought some black pudding.

He was nearly always the one who had to do the shopping, as Samuel got back home so late from the forest. Joel did the cooking, the washing-up and the shopping day after day. But Samuel did the cleaning and washed all the clothes. He did that on Saturday evenings before they sat down to listen to the wireless.

Joel didn't like shopping for food. At the grocer's, Ehnströms Livs, he had to jostle with old women who could never make up their minds what they wanted to buy. If he was unlucky he might bump into the mother of one of his classmates. It was at moments like that he felt annoyed with his own mum, Jenny, who had gone away and left Joel and Samuel. Even if she didn't want to stay with her family, she could at least have made sure they had all the food they would need. She could have filled the house up to the rafters with food. Then Joel wouldn't have needed to keep running to the shops and coping with all those women.

The previous year, however, he had made a big change to the routine. He started shopping only every other day. In addition, he bought the same food for the same weekday every week. Anything to speed things up.

On Mondays they always had black pudding and potatoes. With lingonberries that he and Samuel would pick in the autumn and make into jam.

But this particular Monday, things were not the same as usual at Ehnström's.

Joel noticed that the moment he entered the shop.

There was a new assistant. It was usually Mr. Ehnström himself, or his wife, Klara, who did the serving. Now there was a different woman behind the counter. She was much younger than most of the other women in the shop. Joel had never seen her before. That put him off slightly.

"Black pudding," he said in a firm voice when it was his turn.

The girl behind the counter smiled.

"How much?" she asked.

"Enough for two people," said Joel, his usual response.

"Just think—the lad lives alone with his dad and does all the housework himself," said somebody behind his back.

Joel whipped round. It was a big, fat woman; her face was sweaty. She was the mother of one of the girls in Joel's class. At that moment he hated both the mother and the daughter. It was his classmate who had blabbed about Joel's not having a mother, of course. And then, naturally, this fatty stands here sweating and tells the new shop assistant something that has nothing to do with her.

Joel could feel himself blushing. He always did when he was angry.

"Isn't he a little marvel?" said the fat woman.

Joel hoped she would explode and die on the spot.

The girl behind the counter smiled. But she made no comment. She served the black pudding. Joel paid. All the time he was afraid the fat woman standing behind him and nudging him in the back with her fat belly would say something else about him.

But she didn't.

When Joel emerged into the street, he was still embarrassed. He didn't want to go shopping anymore. He didn't want to be his own mother. But he did want revenge. Needless to say, the fat woman hadn't dropped dead as he'd hoped. It was as he had always said: grown-ups just didn't know what was best for them.

He crossed the street and stood between two lampposts where it was murky. His hands were cold because he didn't have his mittens with him. He stuffed the paper bag containing the black pudding inside his jacket. He should really hurry up now. Dinner ought to be ready by the time Samuel got home. Besides, it was New Year's Eve. He had a lot to prepare before going out that evening.

But he couldn't forget that fat woman who had put him to shame in front of the new shop assistant.

He wondered who the girl was. Could it be Ehnström's daughter? When Joel was handed the black pudding and he paid for it, he'd looked surreptitiously at her. She was younger than he'd first thought. About twenty-five, he'd have said. Although he was bad at guessing people's ages. He sometimes thought that Miss Nederström was ninety, but somebody had told him, to his great surprise, that she wasn't even fifty.

There was something else about the new shop assistant that had made him curious. She sounded different when she talked. She wasn't a local. Although he couldn't be certain, he thought she probably came from Stockholm. The previous summer, a traveling circus had come to town. As usual, Joel had helped to erect the fence and carry chairs in order to get a free ticket. He'd run an errand for one of the circus workers, and bought some coffee. The worker came from Stockholm, and spoke a very distinctive dialect. The new shop assistant at the grocer's spoke in a similar way. As far as he could tell.

His train of thought was broken when the fat woman came out of the shop. Joel gritted his teeth and hoped as hard as he could that she would slip on the steps and kill herself. But she didn't, of course. It was only innocent people who slipped and got hurt. Really bad criminals never did. Nor did fat women who talked about things that didn't concern them.

Joel saw her hang her shopping bag on the handle of a kick sledge. He thought it looked like a Walker on runners. It was painted brown, and there were fancy upturned points at the front of the runners, which was a bit unusual.

Joel memorized what the sledge looked like. He knew where the woman lived. On one of his evening expeditions through the town, he would pee all over it.

He watched her disappear round the corner. She still hadn't burst. Joel hurried home. He felt cold. His hands were white. He thought about the new shop assistant at Ehnström's.

He wasn't quite sure exactly what he thought.

When he got home he took off his boots, and started his work by peeling the potatoes. Then he snuggled down in his bed and massaged his toes. They felt sore. His boots really were too small for him. He wondered whether he ought to limp when Samuel came home. Or maybe he ought to lie down and drag himself over the floor. As if he'd been crippled by the boots. In which case Samuel couldn't very well refuse to buy him a new pair.

He decided to wait until the following day. The boots would still be too small then. He had too many more important things to do tonight.

While he was waiting for the potatoes to boil, he went to the bathroom and examined his face in his dad's shaving mirror. He had got into the habit of doing this over the last year. It was a New Year's resolution he'd made a year ago. He would examine his face in the mirror every afternoon, and see how much he'd changed. But now, after a whole year, he thought he looked exactly the same as before. The shaving mirror couldn't tell him that he'd grown bigger and taller. Nor could it tell him that his feet had become too big for his boots. He supposed it would have been better to have examined his feet in the mirror every day, but surely nobody did that?

Joel tested the potatoes with a fork. Five more minutes. While he was waiting he laid the table. Sometimes he would put out a third plate. Just to see what it would look like. If Mummy Jenny had still been there. He wondered where she would have sat. Between him and his dad? Or in his own place, next to the stove? He decided that was it. She would have been the one to collect the food from the stove.

When everything was ready, the black pudding fried and placed under a lid to keep it warm, and the lingonberry jam fetched from the pantry and put on the table, all he had to do was to wait for Samuel. Joel did what he always did: sat on the window seat and looked down at the street. He'd done that for as long as he could remember. That was the window from which he'd seen that mysterious dog. It was also where he generally sat when he was forced to make a difficult decision. Or when he felt sad.

You could say that the window seat was Joel's home. Just as the glass showcase was the home of the *Celestine*.

Joel's showcase was the window seat. That was his house and his castle.

It was also there that he had realized that something was happening to him. He really was growing bigger. The window seat was starting to feel cramped. There had always been plenty of room, but he had difficulty sitting there now with both his feet up. Especially when he had sore toes.

He was growing up.

The *Celestine* was a model of a ship that would never grow any bigger.

Her master would never become too big to fit inside the case.

Joel tried to work out if it was going to start snowing again. The sky was cloudy. And heavy. Like an awning sagging as a result of all the snow that had fallen on it. It was when the awning split that the snow started to fall down to the ground.

Needless to say, Joel knew that there was no truth in any such thoughts. There was no awning up in the sky. Snow was rain that had frozen and turned into snowflakes.

Warm rain fell in the summer. Cold rain in the winter. But the awning idea was better. Easier to understand.

Then he saw Samuel approaching. A shadow on the other side of the street.

A shadow with a hunched back.

After dinner Joel went to his room and closed the door behind him. He could hear Samuel making coffee, then switching on the wireless to hear the news.

There was a lot Joel needed to prepare. You couldn't make your New Year's resolutions any old way: it had to happen at dead-on midnight.

As he was going to be up late, he lay down on top of his bed and covered himself with a blanket. It would be best if he could manage to sleep for a couple of hours. To be on the safe side, he set his alarm clock for eleven o'clock and put it underneath the blanket.

He could hear a munching noise from inside the wall, right next to his ear. He pressed his cheek against the cold wallpaper. He could now hear the mouse very clearly. It was less than an inch away from him. But it had no idea that Joel's cheek was so close.

Joel tapped on the wall with the knuckle of his hand. The mouse fell silent. Then it started munching again.

Joel continued listening. Before long he was fast asleep.

When the alarm went off, it was some considerable time before Joel came to. When he woke up he remembered his dream: he had been inside the wall, looking for the mouse in a complicated network of caves among the wooden beams and uprights.

But it was all quiet now. The mouse couldn't be heard any longer. The only sound penetrating the wall was Samuel's snoring.

Joel sat up. He still wasn't wide awake. When he stood up he had to push hard with both arms. Then he started to doze off again. Just as his eyes closed he gave a start, as if he had burnt his fingers. He went to the window, opened it slightly and scraped up some snow from the windowsill. Then he took a deep breath and rubbed the snow into his face.

Now he really was awake. He looked out into the night. The sky had become completely clear while he'd been asleep. The stars were twinkling.

He closed the window carefully, got dressed and tiptoed into the kitchen with his rucksack in his hand. He put on his jacket, his scarf and his wooly hat. He had found his mittens while he was waiting for the potatoes to boil. He put on his rucksack, picked up his Wellingtons and slipped silently out the door.

Samuel was asleep. His snores came and went in waves. Joel avoided treading on the steps that creaked, the fourth, fifth and twelfth. Then he opened the front door.

It was cold outside.

He stepped out and looked up at the starry sky.

It really was a genuine New Year's Eve.

Then he opened the gate and set off for the place he had picked out for his ceremony.

He would make his New Year's resolutions in the churchyard.

— THREE —

Before Joel went to the churchyard, he had another important task to complete.

He had made a resolution the year before, but hadn't carried it out. Now he had just one hour left in which to do it.

New Year's resolutions were not things to be taken lightly. It seemed to Joel that a New Year's resolution unkept might turn out to be a New Year's threat. Time was up at midnight. The sands of time had run out. Just as in that hourglass Samuel had bought years ago in some foreign port or other, in a dimly lit little shop smelling of spices.

Joel had kept putting off carrying out this resolution for a whole year. That was something typical of him that he didn't much like. He could promise too much.

Promise himself, and others as well. He had promised the man in the bicycle shop to call in and pay for a puncture repair the same afternoon it had happened. But he'd forgotten. He'd promised Samuel to collect something from the ironmonger's, and he'd forgotten that as well. And it was something Samuel needed for his work in the forest.

Another thing about this resolution was that he regretted having made it. He'd been too hasty. But it seemed to him that New Year's resolutions simply could not be ignored. You had a whole year in which to do what you'd promised yourself to do. But no more. And now there was only one hour left.

He hurried through the silent little town without making a sound.

There was no traffic, no noise at all. Everything was different at night. Shadows and streetlamps. The white snow.

And Joel running through the streets like a man possessed. Now he had come to the Grand Hotel. He turned off to the left, and then to the right. The clock in the church tower was lit up. A quarter past eleven. He passed over the big forecourt in front of the bank and forced his way through the broken fence at the back of the hardware store. Then it was just a question of continuing straight ahead, towards the red-painted, timber-built fire station with the tall tower where the hoses were hung up.

He was taking the same route he took every morning.

He was going to school in the middle of the night.

When he entered the playground he suddenly thought he could hear the bell ringing. There were voices on all sides. Just like it always sounded during the breaks. He even thought he could hear his own voice. That was something he'd rather not listen to. He'd once heard his own voice on Mr. Waltin's tape recorder. Waltin was the editor of the local newspaper, and Joel used to work as a newspaper delivery boy. If Mr. Waltin was in a good mood and you were lucky, he would record your voice and let you listen to it. Joel had been lucky. But he didn't like the sound of his own voice. He spoke through his nose. And his voice was shrill.

But needless to say, he was only imagining all those voices on the playground. He was the only one there. And he was in a hurry.

The worst thing was that he was frightened of what he was going to do. If he was caught breaking into school in the middle of the night, he hoped the earth would open and swallow him up. He would be in trouble for the rest of his life. He preferred not even to think about how Samuel would react.

How on earth could he have made that idiotic New Year's resolution? How could he have been so stupid?

He had been a little kid then. This year such a thought would never have entered his head.

But there was nothing he could do about it. New Year's resolutions could think. They kept track of who had promised what.

He crouched up against the wall of the school and listened. He could hear a car in the far distance. But it didn't come any closer. Soon everything was just as still as before.

Joel had made preparations earlier in the day. At the end of the last lesson, he'd stayed behind in the classroom and when everybody had left, he'd carefully released the catch on one of the windows. He'd jammed a piece of folded paper in the crack at the bottom of the window, so that it wouldn't blow open if a wind got up. He hoped the caretaker hadn't noticed anything. If he had, Joel was in deep trouble.

He ran across the schoolyard to the shedlike building that contained his classroom, took off his mittens and tried the window.

He could move it. The paper was still there. Nobody had noticed that the catch wasn't fastened.

He suddenly gave a start and whipped round. He thought he'd heard something behind him. But there was nothing there. Everything was quiet.

He opened the window and heaved himself up. He had to strain as hard as he could to get high enough to scramble inside.

It was a strange feeling, being in his classroom late at night. The light from the streetlamps cast a ghostly glow over the empty desks. There was still a smell of wet clothes. He sat down at his desk. Put his hand up. Then he went up to the teacher's desk. He tripped over a satchel that somebody had forgotten. The clatter echoed in the silence. He stood still and held his breath. But there was nobody there to hear anything. Everybody was asleep. Apart from the lost soul by the name of Joel Gustafson.

He sat down at Miss Nederström's desk, and looked down at all the pupils' desks in front of him. He looked at his own place.

"Joel Gustafson hasn't been listening to what I said, as usual," he said in an appropriately loud voice.

He stood up and walked to his own desk. Sat down, then stood up again.

"Go and sit on the outhouse roof, Miss Nederström, and don't bother to come down again," he replied.

Then he wished he hadn't. Perhaps there was somebody who could hear him after all? Or a tape recorder hidden somewhere?

Besides, time was nearly up. It must be at least a quarter to twelve. Now he had only fifteen minutes left. He went to the harmonium to the left of the teacher's desk, crouched down by the pedals and groped around with his hand until he located the bellows. He unhooked the connection at the back, then pressed the pedals. No air came.

Tomorrow morning, when Miss Nederström started to play the morning hymn, there wouldn't be a sound. And she wouldn't be able to understand for the life of her what had happened. Nobody would understand it. Apart from Joel.

He clambered out the window again, put the folded piece of paper back in place and closed the window. It squeaked slightly.

At that very moment the church clock started to strike. Three booms. A quarter to twelve. Fifteen minutes to midnight. It had been a close shave, but he'd made it.

The last of last year's New Year's resolutions had been kept. Now he could start thinking about this year's.

He'd left his rucksack in the shadow of the wall. He put it back on, smoothed down the snow under the window so that his footsteps couldn't be seen, and hurried away.

It was five minutes to twelve now. It would soon be New Year's Day. He could see the illuminated clock face up in the tower. Joel had paused by the black wrought-iron gate leading into the churchyard. He shuddered, and noticed that he had a stomachache.

He'd never been in the churchyard after dark before. Even though he was often around town on his bike at night.

But that was where he was going to go now. It was another of his New Year's resolutions from last year: next time, he would announce his new resolutions in the churchyard at midnight. He would walk in through the gate and prove that doing so wouldn't make him die of fright.

He felt cold. Wondered why he had put himself in this

position. But there was no going back. He had to go in among all the gravestones lit up by the moonlight.

You could keep the vampires away with garlic, but there was no known medicine to protect you when you visited a churchyard in the middle of the night.

To be on the safe side, Joel had packed an onion in his rucksack. Even if it didn't help, it could hardly do any harm.

He'd also packed a couple of potatoes. One raw and one boiled. Samuel used to say that there was nothing like potatoes to keep people fit and well. Perhaps that indicated that potatoes had some kind of magical powers?

He checked the clock. Four minutes to midnight. He couldn't wait any longer. He took hold of the handle and opened the gate. The squeaking noise made him shudder. Let's hope it doesn't wake the dead, he thought nervously.

But then he realized: dead people don't wake up. Once you're dead, you're dead. Everything else is just imagination.

He entered the churchyard. One step. Then another. On his left was a gravestone in memory of an old vicar. Died 1783. That was so long ago, it was almost impossible to imagine. But perhaps Samuel was right. There would always be people living here, where the river very nearly formed a circle before continuing its long journey to the sea. And they would eventually die, and be buried in the churchyard.

Joel would have preferred to stand just inside the gate, but he forced himself to continue. Now he had gravestones on all sides. Just ahead, the church loomed like a gigantic beast, fast asleep.

He jumped when the clock started striking twelve. It sounded much louder when he was there in the darkness, all alone.

Now it was time. The last stroke had died away.

Joel closed his eyes tightly. And concentrated hard on his resolutions:

I hereby promise faithfully to live to be a hundred. In order to do that, I must toughen up. I shall start on that this year. I shall learn how to tolerate both cold and heat.

That was his first resolution. He had three. He moved on to number two:

During the year to come I shall find a solution to Samuel's big problem, which is also my big problem. The fact that we never move away from this place. That he doesn't become a sailor again. Before this year is over, I shall have seen the sea for the first time.

That was his second resolution. Now he only had one left. The most difficult one. Because he was afraid that somebody might hear his thoughts, despite everything. Or see what he was thinking by looking at him.

I shall see a naked woman. At some point this coming year.

He thought that one as quickly as possible. His third resolution. So that was that. Now he could leave the churchyard. The dead, who could hear nothing, had been able to hear his New Year's resolutions even so. He couldn't possibly break them now. Standing in a church-yard and promising something was similar to swearing something with your hand on the Bible. As he had read about and seen in the cinema.

He turned round. There was the gate. The streetlamps. The light. It hadn't been necessary to use the onion or the potatoes. Now he could go home and go back to sleep.

That was when he realized he had lost one of his mittens. He knew it must be somewhere close by. It was here, just before he had made his New Year's resolutions, that he had taken his mittens off. He'd packed a box of matches in his rucksack. He took it off and fumbled around for the matches. He lit one and looked around on the ground. It blew out. He lit another one. There was the mitten. He bent down to pick it up. As he did, he happened to glance at the gravestone next to where it was lying. Before the match went out he just had time to register that there was something odd about what it said on the stone. He lit another one. *Lars Olson. Born 1922, died 1936.*

Under that stone was somebody who had only lived to be fourteen years old.

The match burnt out. Joel was panic-stricken. He grabbed his rucksack and ran to the gate. He started pushing it, but it wouldn't move. His heart was pounding. Moreover, he thought he could hear heavy breathing

33

behind him. He pushed as hard as he could. The gate opened. Joel ran for it, without looking round. Kept on running until he could no longer see the church or the churchyard. He stopped under a streetlamp outside the bookshop. Only then did he turn round. There was nobody there.

He continued walking home.

Now he had made his resolutions. That was good. But he wished he hadn't seen that gravestone. It was the fault of that damned mitten of his. Missing mittens always caused problems.

Why could nobody invent mittens that never got lost?

Joel crept in through the front door and tiptoed upstairs. He paused in the kitchen and listened. Samuel was asleep.

A few minutes later, he was in bed. Heat spread slowly through his body. His alarm clock with the luminous hands was on a stool beside his bed.

Half past twelve.

Everything had gone well after all. He would forget about Lars Olson's gravestone. He had another pair of mittens. They needed darning, but if he did that he could wear them. Anyway, he'd made his New Year's resolutions.

The new year had begun.

He had so much to do. If he was going to be able to do it all, he would have to start as early as the next day.

— FOUR —

When Joel woke up next morning, he felt ill. He was hot and sweaty. And he had a sore throat. Samuel came to his room and wondered why he was still in bed.

"I feel awful," said Joel. "I have a sore throat."

Samuel felt his forehead.

"You seem to have a bit of a temperature," he said. "I think you ought to stay at home today."

That was exactly what Joel had hoped to hear. He was really ill. Many a time he'd woken up and wished he'd been ill. Mornings when the last thing he'd wanted to do was to go to school. But needless to say, he'd been unable to find anything at all wrong with himself, no matter how much he'd squeezed and poked at his body.

"Will you be all right on your own?" Samuel asked.

Joel wondered what Samuel would have done if he'd

said no. Would he have stayed at home and not gone to work? He couldn't have done that. Samuel didn't earn much money. They couldn't afford for him to miss a single day's work in the forest.

"I'll manage OK," said Joel. "I'm only a little bit ill."

"Wrap something warm round your neck," Samuel said. "And I think we'd better lay the cat fur over your feet."

Joel smiled. There was no cat fur. But there was a little Arabian carpet that Samuel had bought ages ago in some Mediterranean port or other. It was no bigger than a doormat. But when Joel was a little lad, Samuel had told him stories about its magical properties. If you laid it over your feet when you were ill, you would be cured straightaway. In those days Joel had believed it was true. But he didn't any longer.

Even so, he was pleased that Samuel went to fetch the little mat and placed it over the bottom of the bed. Even if it didn't have any magical properties, at least it made your feet warm.

"Drink plenty of water," Samuel said. "Do you want me to open the blind?"

Yes, Joel did. And the roller blind was raised.

Samuel set off for work.

Joel lay in his bed, listening to the silence. Nothing could make as much noise as a silent room. There was a creaking in the walls, and a swishing from the water pipes.

He swallowed several times, as a sort of test. It hurt. But not all that much.

He thought about what had happened last night. The New Year's resolutions he'd made, which had been witnessed by all those dead people.

The fact that he'd dropped his mitten in front of Lars Olson's gravestone didn't mean a thing. Even if Lars Olson had died at the age of fourteen, Joel's name was Joel and not Lars Olson. Joel had made a solemn resolution to the effect that he would toughen himself up and live to be a hundred. The year that would eventually be carved on his gravestone was 2045.

Joel was aware that lots of people would no doubt think it was a childish resolution. Lots of people who didn't understand.

OK, maybe I am childish, Joel thought. But I don't know what I ought to do in order not to be. To be different.

He went to the kitchen and poured himself a glass of water. He put it at the side of his alarm clock. It would soon be time for the first lesson to start.

And then he remembered. The harmonium! He'd forgotten all about it.

He felt a pain in his stomach. The moment Miss Nederström started to pedal and no sound emerged from the organ, she would know that it was Joel who was responsible. Joel Gustafson, who wasn't sitting at his desk.

Oh, hell! Joel thought. Why did I have to be ill today of all days?

Then he tried to think it through, totally calm. He had left no traces. Nobody could know that he'd been responsible. The bellows could have become disconnected as a result of normal wear and tear.

Joel tried to convince himself that maybe it wasn't all that bad. He also hoped that he wasn't the only one to feel ill that morning.

He felt tired. And as Samuel had said, he had a bit of a temperature.

He pulled the covers up to his chin.

He was soon fast asleep.

When he woke up, it was ten o'clock. He swallowed. It still hurt, but he felt better even so. He didn't feel quite as hot as he had been. Perhaps the mat at the bottom of his bed had helped after all? You could never be certain about things that sailors bought in mysterious shops in foreign ports.

Joel sat up, emptied his glass of water and noted that he didn't feel hungry. He propped up the cushion behind his back and started thinking. Or maybe he was just dreaming? Very often he wasn't at all sure what the difference was. Thoughts and dreams came from the same place. From somewhere inside yourself, from an underground cave system deep down in your head. Thinking was harder than dreaming. You had to make an effort in order to think. Dreaming was the opposite. You couldn't do it if you made an effort. Just now his instinct was to let dreams have the upper hand. If he started to think, he would soon start worrying about whether Miss Nederström had realized that it was Joel who had disconnected the bellows from the pedals.

And perhaps, despite everything, he had left some traces behind to prove that he'd been in the classroom in the middle of the night? Perhaps drops of water had dripped from his boots and formed the word *Joel* on the floor?

So, it was all down to dreaming. Joel chose between the dreams he used to have while he was awake. He couldn't pick and choose between the dreams he had when he was asleep, but he could when he was awake.

The ship, he thought. The brig *Three Lilies*. The sister ship of the *Celestine*, resplendent in its showcase. Captain Gustafson is confined to his cabin, suffering badly from some tropical fever or other. But he hasn't yet given up the ghost. He's still in command of his ship....

They hadn't set eyes on land for more than fifty days. The sails were drooping down round the masts. Supplies of fresh water had almost run out. All they had left to eat was moldy ship's biscuits. It was becoming difficult to keep the crew under control. They wanted to turn back. Ahead was the abyss: the ship would be hurled over the edge of the world, and sink down to the very bottom of an unknown ocean. Soon there would be no fresh water left to drink. But Captain Gustafson had a map inside his head that revealed itself to him every night. He knew as a result that they would soon strike land. An unknown continent. And they would step ashore in paradise itself.

They were there now. After sixty-four days at sea. A tropical island. Parrots were chattering in the trees.

Captain Gustafson is still ill, and is carried ashore.

Somebody comes to greet him. At first he can't make out who it is. Then he sees that it is a naked woman. He seems to recognize her. Where has he seen her before? And then it dawns on him. The woman walking towards him along the sand, the naked woman, is somebody he's seen in one of the magazines Otto hands round behind the bicycle sheds during the breaks.

Joel woke up with a start. This had never happened to him before. A naked woman coming towards him in a dream. Not as unexpectedly as this, in any case. Before, he'd always been able to dictate who turned up in his dreams. But not this time; she'd come of her own accord.

There was something else that was different. It eventually dawned on him that she wasn't only like somebody he'd seen in one of Otto's magazines: she had reminded him of the new shop assistant in Ehnström's grocery store.

Joel tried to escape back into his dream. Closed his eyes and leaned back on the pillows. But no matter what he did, he couldn't get back there. His dream had gone away. And he couldn't get back in touch with it.

But he knew that it was connected to his New Year's resolutions. He knew that in the coming year, he would see a real naked woman.

Something had happened during the past year. Something that had shaken his whole world to its foundations.

Something inside him. Hatches that had opened up, secret doors that had been flung open wide.

Feelings were like doors. Joel knew that. Sorrow had its own room; so did disappointment, and happiness. Life was like a long corridor. Every door you walked past concealed something you could choose to accept. Or reject. If you knocked on the door and went in. Always assuming you were allowed in. But doors you hoped would remain closed could also open unexpectedly.

It was all to do with Otto's magazines. Where more or less naked women were climbing up ladders, or sitting on balconies in front of some photographer or others who snapped and snapped away. He couldn't say whether what was happening inside him was good or not. But it worried him. He was on fire.

During breaks Otto often went on and on and on about how things stood. He *hissed* when he spoke. Not too loud, not too soft. Just so that those gathered round him could hear. No girls, only boys. And Otto hissed. About big girls' secrets. And Joel had always listened carefully. But there again, he didn't trust Otto. Not just because they had more or less always been enemies, Otto was always bragging. But on the other hand, Joel could never be absolutely sure. You could only be sure when you knew yourself. And not always then.

Joel thought about the woman in his dream. How she had walked towards him. Captain Joel Gustafson had dared to look at her. But the one having the dream, Joel

41

Gustafson with a sore throat, had looked away. He hadn't really dared to look at her, not even in his dream. He hadn't really had much more than a glimpse.

Joel had chosen that word carefully. A *glimpse*. Something you nearly saw, not quite. And that was exactly what the woman had been.

But he had seen something. All the unknown things that worried him.

And she had been very much like the new shop assistant at Ehnström's. The one who spoke with a Stockholm accent, and hadn't become an old woman yet.

Then it dawned on Joel. He was ill in bed, but he knew. The New Year's resolution he had made, about seeing a naked woman: it would be Ehnström's shop assistant. With no clothes on. But goodness only knew how he would be able to manage that.

Nevertheless, it was a step in the right direction. He knew now who he had picked out. Or rather, who the dream had chosen for him.

He noticed that the dream had made him hungry. And his throat was hardly sore anymore. He went to the pantry and fetched what was left of the black pudding from the previous evening. Cold black pudding was not exactly tasty. But when you were really hungry, it didn't much matter what you ate. He prepared a plate of black pudding and jam. Then he clambered up onto the window seat. A car drove past, then another one shortly afterwards. Fat old women were shuffling along the pavements, trying not to slip. No doubt they were heading for Ehnströms Livs to do their shopping. And none of them saw Joel sitting on the window seat, hoping they would slip and fall down.

Joel ate. He was really hungry. Then he went back to his room. Wondered if Lars Olson, lying dead out there in the churchyard, had ever eaten black pudding. Had Captain Joel Gustafson ever been forced to survive on any of his long voyages with nothing to eat but cold black pudding?

He banished the thought as he went back to bed and snuggled down under the cover. What he would most have liked to do was to continue dreaming about the woman who had come towards him on the beach. But he had other New Year's resolutions to think about. And besides, there was a long day ahead of him. It would be many hours before Samuel came back from the forest.

He was going to live to be a hundred. Live until at least 2045. If he was going to live that long, he'd have to toughen himself up. But in the world he lived in, there were no giants to fight.

The only thing was winter: the snow and the cold.

Yes, winter would be the giant he would challenge and overcome. He would show that he was stronger than the cold.

And he knew what he was going to do. As soon as he was fit again, he would begin.

He would start sleeping outdoors.

There was an old bed in the woodshed at the bottom of the garden. That was what he would use. When Samuel had fallen asleep Joel would take his bedclothes and make up a bed outside the shed. To start with, he would dress in outdoor clothes and boots. But when he'd got used to it and become tough, he would only wear his pajamas.

He felt a stabbing pain in his stomach at the very thought.

Sleeping in a bed out there in the snow.

But he'd made the resolution. The dead had heard him make it. Lars Olson had been a witness to Joel's New Year's resolutions. There was no getting away from it.

He curled up under the blanket. Swallowed. His throat felt rough and jagged. Like a piece of wood he'd sawn up in his woodworking lesson. But at least it didn't seem to be getting any worse.

Then he thought about his third resolution. How he was going to devote the coming year to solving the biggest of all the problems he faced. To persuading Samuel to dig his axe deep down into some tree stump or other and leave it there once and for all, to take out his old suitcases and sailor's kitbag from the wardrobe, and say: The time has come. Now we're going to the sea. The waves are waiting for us.

The waves are waiting for us.

Joel could feel a surge of hot blood running through him. The waves were waiting for them somewhere in the far distance. But would they wait forever?

Joel knew that there were only two possibilities. The first was that he do something that brought such disgrace on himself and Samuel that it was impossible for them to stay in this place any longer. That was option number one. They would have to run away.

The other was that Joel find a way of earning vast amounts of money. So that Samuel no longer needed to chop down lots of trees in order to earn enough money for them to be able to eat.

But how could he possibly earn as much money as that? He was thirteen years of age. Just a young brat. And young brats didn't earn any money.

Even so, he had a few ideas.

One was to become Sweden's youngest rock idol. A Snow Elvis.

Another was to sell trailers. He'd heard all about that. Selling trailers was an excellent way of getting rich quick.

His train of thought was broken. Something had disturbed him. Then he looked out the window and jumped out of bed.

It had started snowing again. A mass of snowflakes were cascading down to the ground.

— FIVE —

Miss Nederström looked at Joel.

It was the following day. When Joel was feeling fit again.

But the look she gave him didn't suggest that she had discovered a secret. She simply asked him if he'd been ill. And he said he had. They had already sung the morning hymn by then. Joel had held his breath when Miss Nederström sat down at the harmonium and started pedaling. If the sound that emerged was not musical notes, he would faint. He grabbed hold of the desk with both hands. As if he'd been in a boat as a big wave was approaching. His classmate Eva-Lisa, the Greyhound, was standing beside him, grinning. But there was no way she could know. She usually grinned at anything slightly different. Joel grabbing tight hold of his desk was enough for that.

But Miss Nederström showed no sign of suspecting him. That was the main thing. So Joel's secret visit to his classroom would remain a mystery. Unless he himself decided to reveal what had happened. Perhaps on his ninetieth birthday, in 2035. But Miss Nederström would already be dead by then. Lying in the churchyard under a heavy stone, just like Lars Olson.

Then the school day began. And it began well. The first lesson was geography, and that had always been Joel's best subject. Especially if Miss Nederström talked about far-distant countries and people. But that day it was about Scandinavia. That wasn't as enjoyable. Even so, Joel listened carefully. It always seemed to him that Miss Nederström also bucked up when they had geography.

That morning he was suddenly struck by the amazing thought that she had once been young as well. Had sat at a school desk just like Joel. And perhaps she had thought that geography was her favorite subject.

That was one of the hardest things for Joel to cope with. Imagining old people being the same age as he was. And that applied not least to Samuel. Joel had sometimes looked at pictures of Samuel as a boy about the same age as himself. He could see that it was Samuel. But it was hard. It somehow seemed to be somebody else he was looking at. When Joel looked at those pictures of Samuel, he wondered how he was going to change as he grew up. What would he see in the mirror in fifty years' time? Not to mention a hundred? He imagined himself going to the photographer's in 2044, the year before he might be going to die. An old man with a long white beard. But without a hunched back. That was something he was never going to get, as long as he lived. He had made up his mind about that. That New Year's resolution would last for the whole of his life, and be repeated every year.

Time passed quickly. When they started the day with geography, it was as if the whole school day braced itself and then shot off over a surface of smooth, shiny ice. Even the boring religious studies lesson could have the occasional exciting moment. This particular time Miss Nederström talked about John the Baptist, who'd had his head cut off and placed on a plate. And Salome danced and was given the head as a reward. Miss Nederström told them that Salome had been very beautiful, and had danced wearing transparent veils. Joel reckoned that must mean she had been more or less naked. Or transparent through and through. The Greyhound giggled. Joel assumed that must mean he was right.

He sat watching the Greyhound without her noticing. She had started to change. Developed breasts. Joel often found it hard not to take hold of her. Especially her breasts. Sometimes, when he leaned over to reach something, he tried to brush against her. But she was on her guard. Not only could the Greyhound run faster than anybody else, she could also growl and show her teeth.

Joel started dreaming. About the new shop assistant at the grocer's, dancing behind the counter, dressed in transparent veils. But the fat old ladies didn't see a thing. It was only Joel who noticed what was happening. Then Ehnström himself appeared behind the counter. On a tray that usually held strings of sausages was a head. Still the fat old ladies didn't see a thing. Only Joel knew what was going on. The head looked like that of Stationmaster Knif, and was still wearing his uniform cap.

He still hadn't stopped dreaming when school was over for the day. Somebody asked if he wanted to go and play in the horse dealer's paddock. There might be enough snow to make a slide. Joel would have loved to go, but he said no even so. There was something he had to do that couldn't wait.

Joel stayed in the playground until the Greyhound had gone home. The person he was going to visit lived in the same block of flats as she did. He didn't want her to know that he was going there. She would only start gossiping about it, and she was as good at gossiping as she was at running.

Joel walked up the hill towards the place where the musician and womanizer Kringström lived. Kringström was the person he was going to visit. He was bald and fat and had his own orchestra. Joel had been to see him the previous year. He'd wanted to learn to play the saxophone. He could still recall how Kringström had stared at him, with his glasses pushed up onto his forehead, surprised to hear that Joel didn't want to play the guitar like everybody else.

But now Joel had changed his mind. That was why he was on the way to Kringström's flat.

A rock idol had to be able to play the guitar.

He continued up the hill. There was no sign of the Greyhound. He couldn't see her anywhere ahead of him.

He still wasn't quite sure what he was going to do, become a rock idol or a trailer salesman. Presumably being a rock idol was more fun. Prancing round a stage with a guitar in your hands. Singing "Hound Dog" into a microphone. And in front of the stage a cheering and whooping mass of people, most of them girls who were dying to pull off your clothes or handfuls of hair.

But there again, he imagined it would be hard going, never being left in peace. Always having to be photographed. Never having time to sit back on his bed, dreaming.

He wondered if a rock idol would ever have time to act like a child again. That worried him. He'd have difficulty coping with that.

Selling trailers was different altogether. It was actually Samuel who'd put the idea into his head. They'd been having dinner in the kitchen. Fried herring, Joel could still recall. He'd ventured to ask Samuel if they'd ever be able to afford a motorcar.

"I doubt it," Samuel had said. "But you might be able to hit upon a way of earning lots of money."

Joel hadn't risen to the bait.

"I suppose you earned a lot of money when you were a sailor?"

"No way!" said Samuel. "But we used to spend a lot of time at sea, where there was nothing to spend our money on. So we'd saved a fair bit by the time we came back ashore."

Joel could see that as his dad said that, he started thinking about Jenny. He'd met Joel's mother while he was a sailor. Samuel's face clouded over. It seemed as if Joel's dad was floating away into the clouds. Maybe he looked a bit angry as well. Joel sometimes wondered if Samuel also hated Mummy Jenny—because she'd put him to shame by running away.

Joel changed the subject. He went back to what they'd started with. Money. How could you best earn a lot of money.

"Tell me who earns lots of money," he said.

"Trailer salesmen," said Samuel.

Joel was surprised by the reply. But Samuel went on to say:

"Ten years from now, every Swede will have a trailer to hitch onto the back of their car. Trailer salesmen are going to get rich."

But we won't be buying a trailer, Joel thought. Or at

least, if we do, Samuel and I will have to become horses and pull it.

What's the point of having a trailer if you can't afford a car?

As usual at such moments, Joel felt very angry. His anger was always lurking in the background, to emerge whenever he thought about how little money they had. He and Samuel were poverty-stricken. Despite the fact that there were supposed to be no poor people in Sweden anymore. But then his anger was transformed into a guilty conscience. Samuel toiled and slaved for all he was worth. He couldn't possibly try harder than he did.

After that conversation in the kitchen Joel spent ages thinking over what Samuel had said. That was how they would be able to afford a car. If Joel sold enough trailers, they'd be able to afford it. They wouldn't have to pull the trailer themselves.

But it was only now, when he'd made his New Year's resolution, that he started to think seriously about the matter. He'd have to make up his mind. Rock idol or trailer salesman. It would be a difficult choice to make.

There were lots of difficulties. But obviously, the main one was that Joel still wasn't even fourteen. Perhaps there was a law saying that anybody who wasn't allowed to ride a moped wasn't allowed to sell trailers either. Perhaps also there was an age limit for rock idols. How old had Elvis been when he first started? Joel decided to ask Kringström. If anybody knew, he ought to. Even if everybody knew that he hated rock 'n' roll, and preferred to play something slow and relaxed like a foxtrot.

Joel had reached the top of the hill. There was the block of flats that Kringström lived in. Still no sign of the Greyhound. Joel noted that Kringström's big black van was parked outside the front door. That meant he was at home. Nobody had ever seen Kringström walking through the streets if he could avoid it. If he had to go anywhere, he always took the van. There was a corner shop over the road from his front door. Kringström even went there by van.

Joel walked up the stairs and rang the doorbell. Kringström answered it. As usual, he had his glasses pushed up onto his forehead.

"You were the one who said he wanted to learn how to play the saxophone," he said, and was obviously offended. "But nothing came of it."

Joel had prepared an answer.

"The dentist said that I shouldn't play wind instruments."

There wasn't a jot of truth in that, of course. There was nothing wrong with Joel's teeth. But Kringström seemed to believe him. It hadn't been difficult for Joel to lie. There were different kinds of lies: white lies and black ones. And then some that Joel thought were gray. This was a gray lie. It didn't affect anybody, and it solved the problem. And it also closed down unnecessary conversation even before it had started.

"I want to learn how to play the guitar instead," Joel said.

"I thought as much," said Kringström. "That's what I thought a year ago."

Kringström let him in. Joel remembered the flat from last year. It was like stepping into a music shop that somebody lived in. There were records everywhere. Mainly 78 rps. But some new LPs had arrived since Joel had been there before. Kringström slumped down into a shabby old armchair and pointed to the other chair. That was for Joel to sit on. As far as he could see, there were no other chairs in the flat, apart from a Windsor-style chair in the kitchen. But on the other hand, there was an apparently infinite number of music stands scattered over the flat in every conceivable place. There was even one in the bathroom. Kringström evidently liked to practice new music all the time. Even when he was on the lavatory.

"What did you say your name was?" Kringström asked.

"Joel Gustafson."

Kringström looked surprised. So he'd forgotten.

"And you want to learn to play the guitar?"

"I've been thinking about a career as a rock idol."

Kringström stared at him in astonishment.

"You mean to say you regard that screeching and whining as a career?"

"All Elvis Presley does is sing."

Kringström gestured impatiently with one hand.

"Don't talk to me about that man," he said. "He ruins young people's taste for music."

Joel realized it would be best not to protest. He didn't want to risk Kringström's throwing him out. The most important thing was learning to play the guitar.

"So you want to be a rock idol," said Kringström in disgust. "And what had you thought of calling yourself?"

"Snow Elvis," said Joel without hesitation.

"Good Lord," said Kringström, shaking his head.

"But first and foremost, I want to learn to play the guitar," Joel said.

"I'll think about it," said Kringström. "Come back in a few days' time when I've had time to think about it."

Kringström had other things to do now. Joel left the flat and went back down the hill. At least the worst was over now. With a bit of luck Kringström wouldn't turn him down. Before too long Joel would also be able to winkle out of him all the secrets you needed to know in order to become a rock idol. Not least how old Elvis Presley had been when he'd made his debut.

He speeded up as he walked down the hill. There was something else he wanted to do before going home to prepare dinner. He wanted to call in at Ehnströms Livs to make sure that the new shop assistant was still there. That she hadn't simply been something he'd dreamt about.

As usual there were lots of old women jostling with each other inside the shop. But it didn't matter today, as Joel wasn't going to buy anything.

She was still there. And now that he observed her from a distance, he could see that she was beautiful. He could very well imagine her dancing in transparent veils. He could feel his body becoming excited at the thought. All the strange things going on inside him that he still hadn't managed to work out. Sooner or later he'd have to talk to Samuel about it. Even if he wasn't at all sure that his dad would be able to give him any answers.

But the shop assistant was still there. He still didn't know what she was called. But he'd find out. And where she lived as well.

One of the fat women bumped into him.

"Mind what you're doing," she said angrily. "Do you have to stand right behind me?"

"You're nothing but a Hound Dog," said Joel cheekily. Then he marched out of the shop.

He hurried home. It had been a good day. He'd done everything he'd planned to do.

The very next day he would start shadowing Ehnström's new shop assistant.

But before that he had another important thing to do.

He must meet Gertrud. The young woman who lived on the other side of the river. And didn't have a nose.

He would go and see her that very same evening.

— SIX —

The railway bridge loomed ahead of Joel.

It was lurking there like a petrified dinosaur. The moonlight glistened in the enormous iron arches.

Not so long ago Joel had tried to climb up one of the arches and gotten stuck. In the end, Samuel had come to the rescue.

Joel shuddered at the thought. If he'd fallen, he would no longer be alive. He'd be like Lars Olson. A skeleton six feet down in the cold earth, with a stone over his head. *Joel Gustafson. Died at the age of eleven.*

He was on his way over the bridge to Gertrud's house. He both wanted and didn't want to think about death. If you thought about it, it was like beckoning it to come. You shouldn't fondle death like you stroked a cat. You should be as wary of it as of a lion in the jungle. But at the same time, the thoughts insisted on forcing their way into his mind. It was difficult to keep them out.

Joel had decided that death was more difficult to understand than life—which was complicated enough. It wasn't possible to imagine yourself as nothing. To think that you could no longer think.

And moreover, you'd be dead for such a long time. That was the hardest thing of all. Lars Olson had already been dead for twenty years. That was longer than Joel had been alive. But there were lots of people who'd been dead for hundreds of years.

If only you didn't need to be dead for so long, Joel thought as he contemplated the railway bridge.

Then it might have been tolerable.

He looked up at the moon. It was seven o'clock. He'd had dinner with Samuel. Now he was on his way to Gertrud's. It was several weeks since he'd seen her last.

He braced himself and started running over the bridge. It was easier to get up speed if he imagined that he was being chased. There were lots of possible pursuers he could think of.

He imagined a cavalry of fat old women riding behind him on horseback, wielding their carrier bags like swords and clubs.

He came to the abutment on the other side of the river. The fat old women disappeared from his mind. He turned onto a little road that followed the river to the left, and came to Gertrud's house in its overgrown garden. It contained a rowan tree and some currant bushes. Her windows were lit up. She was at home.

Joel got his breath back before pulling the leather strap hanging outside the door. A music box started playing inside the hall. That was the signal they had agreed on. Then he heard Gertrud shouting for him to come in.

Joel didn't know how many times he'd visited Gertrud's house, but it was a lot. The first time was that unfortunate night when he and Ture had dug up a frozen anthill and thrown it through her kitchen window. But that was a long time ago. Ture didn't live here anymore. Gertrud and Joel had become friends. Not all the time. They had fallen out the previous year, when Joel had tried to find a husband for Gertrud. But that was all over now. All done and dusted.

Gertrud was a remarkable person. It wasn't simply that she didn't have a nose. Only a hole in her face that she hid behind a handkerchief. Or a red clown's nose when she was in the mood. She had lost her nose as a result of an operation that had gone wrong. Now she lived by herself in this house on the other side of the river from Joel. She had turned thirty, and sometimes told Joel she was beginning to feel old.

Gertrud was like no other person Joel knew. He knew that people used to talk about her behind her back. About her wearing strange clothes that she made herself. About her having a stuffed hare in a birdcage and a toy train in an aquarium. But most of all about her saying whatever came into her head, and what she thought about things. Despite the fact that it was usually exactly the opposite of what other people thought.

But it seemed to Joel that Gertrud was a difficult person. He sometimes thought that whatever she did, she went too far. Joel was always scared of not being like everybody else. What he did and thought when he was on his own was one thing. But when you were with other people you shouldn't draw attention to yourself.

Gertrud was the best friend he had.

He wasn't really happy about that. He would have preferred to have a different best friend. One who had a nose, at least.

But that was the way it was. And Gertrud always listened to what he had to say. She didn't laugh at him—not in a malicious way in any case—when he said something silly. Which he thought he did far too often.

This evening Joel had decided to tell Gertrud about his New Year's resolutions.

But maybe not all three. He was still a bit doubtful as to whether he should tell her about Ehnström's new shop assistant. The one who had already started dancing inside Joel's head, wearing nothing but transparent veils. Joel wasn't really sure how she would react. That was the only thing he and Gertrud had never talked about. Other women.

Gertrud was sitting curled up on her orange-colored sofa, reading the Bible. Joel had never really understood what it meant, being religious. All that stuff about God was some-thing he only thought about now and again. Strangely enough, it was usually when he didn't have any money. As if that were God's fault. Not having a krona for a cinema ticket.

But just now his New Year's resolutions were more im-portant.

Gertrud put down her Bible. Today she had a checked handkerchief over the hole where her nose had once been. She had rolled it up into a ball and pressed it into the hole.

"I thought you'd forgotten all about me," she said. "I haven't seen you for ages."

"There's so much to do for school," Joel said.

Which was nearly true. But not quite. A few weeks had gone by without his giving Gertrud a single thought.

"But anyway, here you are," she went on. "And that means, of course, that you have something on your mind. Is that right?"

Joel nodded. Then he told her about his New Year's resolutions. She listened, with her head on one side and her chin resting on her hand, as usual.

For the moment Joel didn't say anything about Ehnström's new shop assistant.

"Is there an age limit?" he asked. "For being a rock idol? Or a trailer salesman?"

"It might be possible to be too old," she said, "but hardly too young."

"How old was Elvis when he started singing?" Joel

asked. He knew that Gertrud liked Elvis Presley. They had sometimes listened to his records together, and tried to work out what the words meant. It was often difficult. It seemed as if the songs weren't really about anything at all.

"I expect Elvis started singing when he was rocking around inside his mother's stomach."

Joel wasn't at all pleased by that answer. It was far too vague.

"But what about later? After he'd been born?"

"I expect he's been singing for the whole of his life."

Joel realized that Gertrud didn't have a better answer to give him. So he moved on to trailers. He explained how that was really Samuel's idea.

"It could well be true," she said. "But I don't think it sounds like a lot of fun, wandering around a big parking lot crammed full of trailers on display. And trying to sell them. Where are you going to get the money to buy them?"

"I'm not going to buy them. I'm going to sell them."

"But you've got to have something to sell, surely? And before you can sell it, you have to buy it."

Joel hadn't thought of that. Presumably nobody was going to give him any trailers on the strength of his paying for them later?

That settled it. He didn't need to hesitate anymore.

He would become a rock idol. He told Gertrud how he'd already been to see Kringström. First he would learn to play the guitar, and then he'd start practicing singing.

"I didn't know you were a good singer," she said tentatively.

"Elvis isn't a good singer," Joel declared. "But he sings very loud."

She nodded hesitantly.

"But surely, he does sing quite well, doesn't he?"

"But most of all, very loud."

Joel didn't want to go into that any further. Not just now, at least. When he'd learnt to play the guitar and practiced a few songs, she could listen.

She asked if he would like some juice. He would. They went together into her big kitchen. A strange thing about this house was that it had two kitchens, even though it wasn't very big. But that was the way Gertrud wanted it. Just like the way she slept in different beds.

One kitchen was for when she was only a bit hungry. The big one was for when she threw a party and had visitors.

Joel watched her pouring out the juice. He thought that Gertrud could be very pretty. If only she had a nose. And wore proper clothes. Like everybody else. Instead of all those peculiar skirts she made herself.

Joel suddenly found himself seeing only her nose that didn't exist. And all her strange clothes.

He didn't know where the feeling came from, but now he thought she was revolting.

She handed him the glass of juice. He took it.

"What's the matter?" she asked.

"Nothing."

"I can see that something's bothering you."

"Don't talk such garbage!"

Now it hit him even more strongly. The feeling that Gertrud was revolting. And was a person who could see right through him. Read his thoughts. What did they call somebody like that? A witch, that was what she was. But without the long nose. Gertrud was even worse. She didn't have a nose at all.

Then everything went very quickly. He flung the glass of juice at the wall. It shattered and the juice splashed all over Gertrud's clothes. Some of it even landed on the handkerchief she had stuffed into the hole where her nose should have been. But Joel didn't see that. He'd already turned on his heel, left the kitchen, grabbed his jacket and boots and carried them out into the garden. He had palpitations and didn't know what had come over him. He struggled and cursed as he tried to fasten his boots. All the time he kept looking round. But Gertrud didn't come after him. When he'd finished tying his laces the sweat was pouring off him. He ran off as fast as he could. Not until he'd reached the middle of the railway bridge did he pause to catch his breath. Steam was coming out of his mouth. His sweat was starting to freeze and made him feel cold. He was trembling. But the main problem was inside him. What had he done? Why had he hurled that glass of juice at the wall? He'd gone to visit Gertrud, who was his friend. He'd wanted her to answer some of the questions that were bothering him. But when she'd asked him a question he'd thrown a glass at her wall.

He regretted it now. He was still out of breath. And very cold. The sweat was pricking at his skin like needles underneath his sweater. He stared down into the black water. There was no ice yet, but the water had started to thicken.

I'll jump, he thought. I can't handle this. I can't see Gertrud ever again. Why did I do that?

But he didn't jump. He remembered that Gertrud had once tried to commit suicide. In this same river. And she really did have a reason, not having a nose.

It seemed to him that he ought to go back to her place right away. She couldn't have understood what had happened either. But maybe she could explain it for him. Explain what he had done.

But he didn't go back. He was far too cowardly for that. He shouted up into the sky.

"Because I'm too much of a coward. Joel Gustafson's a lily-livered coward."

Then he walked home. He was so cold, he was shivering. His teeth were chattering.

When he got to the flat he found Samuel sitting by the wireless. A squeaky voice was holding forth. Samuel had fallen asleep. His head was resting on his chest. Mouth wide open. Joel tiptoed past. He would have preferred Samuel not to wake up just now. In fact, he would have liked the whole world to be asleep. He closed the door to his room, got undressed and snuggled down into bed. He slowly began to thaw out. He closed his eyes and tried to convince himself that it was all a figment of his imagination. He hadn't in fact hurled a glass at Gertrud's kitchen wall. She wasn't upset.

But it wasn't possible to conjure it all away. He was able to think of something else for a few brief moments, but then it all came back again. The kitchen. Gertrud's question. His curse. The glass thrown at the wall.

He had a stomachache now.

There were moments in Joel Gustafson's life when he simply didn't know what to do next.

This was one of those moments.

He could hear that Samuel had woken up. He'd switched off the wireless. Joel pulled the cover over his head and pretended to be fast asleep. Samuel opened the door just a few inches. Listened. Then closed it again.

But Joel was awake.

If only he'd been able, he'd have left his body there and gone away. But human beings couldn't shed their skin. Only snakes could do that.

He didn't know what had happened. If he thought that Gertrud was repulsive, it wasn't her fault. She wasn't the one who had cut off her own nose.

Samuel fell asleep. His snores came booming through the wall. Just now it was hard to think about the new shop assistant at Ehnströms Livs. Or about how he would soon be beginning a new career as Sweden's youngest rock idol. Perhaps even the youngest in the world.

He tried to fall asleep and forget all about what had happened. But he couldn't. So he got out of bed and went over to the window. The sky was clear and full of stars. Then he looked down at the street, where the lone streetlamp lit up the snow. That was where he had seen the mysterious dog run past several years ago.

But then he felt a stab in his chest. There was some-body standing there in the shadows, at the very edge of the light cast by the streetlamp. At first he thought he was imagining it, but then he was certain. There was somebody standing there, staring up at his window.

Then it dawned on him who it was.

It was Gertrud.

— SEVEN —

It had never happened before.

Gertrud had never stood by that streetlamp before. Neither by day nor, like now, at night. When Joel first saw her, he thought she was a mirage. Something that could be seen, but didn't really exist. But she was still there, moving slightly, until she came within range of the streetlamp. Now she was very clear. Joel stood with his face pressed up against the cold windowpane. It was Gertud, all right. And she was gazing up at his window. But he knew that she couldn't possibly know that he was there. The room was in darkness. He could see her. But she couldn't see him.

There was something frightening about her standing out there in the night. Joel had the feeling that he was looking at the last person left alive in the world. This must be what the doomsday that Miss Nederström kept going on about looked like. The last person alive was standing underneath a streetlamp, late at night in an insignificant little northern Swedish town.

Joel couldn't imagine greater loneliness than this.

Then it was clear to him that he would have to go down and fetch her. No human being could be allowed to be as lonely as she seemed to be. He put on a pair of pants, and a sweater over his pajamas, and forced his bare feet into a pair of Wellingtons in the kitchen. Samuel was asleep. He was snoring loudly.

When Joel emerged into the street he suddenly felt embarrassed. But it was too late now. She had already seen him come out of the front door. He couldn't turn back now, or pretend that he hadn't seen her.

They were standing on opposite sides of the street. Everything was silent. Nothing but night and the starry sky. Joel could feel the cold sneaking down into his boots. He walked hesitantly across the street, more or less forcing himself to move.

"Why are you standing here?" he asked.

"You threw a glass at my kitchen wall," said Gertrud. "These things happen, I've done it myself. But I didn't understand why. That's why I've come here."

"I'd nearly fallen asleep," Joel said.

Why did he say that? Couldn't he have thought of something better?

But what he said next made him even more surprised.

69

"Let's go up to the flat," he said. "I don't have any socks on. It's cold."

Things were getting worse and worse.

He couldn't take her up to the flat with him. What would happen if Samuel woke up? But there again, it was too late. He couldn't take it back now.

"Maybe you've got to get back home?" asked Joel tentatively.

"I've got all the time in the world," she said. "Besides, I've never seen what your home is like."

"We'd better be as quiet as possible. So that we don't wake Samuel up."

They were inside the house now.

"Which steps creak?" she asked.

"The fourth, fifth and twelfth," Joel told her.

They entered the flat without making a sound. It was the first time Joel had ever had a visitor in the middle of the night.

"It smells good," she whispered as they stood in the kitchen.

"It smells of fried herring," said Joel.

Samuel snored. They went into Joel's room and closed the door. He placed his finger over his lips.

"Sound carries in here," he said.

"Old houses have good ears," she said, sitting down on his bed.

Joel felt uneasy. He didn't want Samuel to wake up. To come into his room and find Gertrud there.

Now those thoughts started coming back again.

He could see her nose that didn't exist.

He had been visited by a nose that didn't exist.

He'd have preferred it to be Ehnström's new shop assistant visiting him. Sitting there on his bed. Sitting there wearing ordinary clothes, and speaking with a Stockholm accent.

But it was Gertrud who'd turned up.

It seemed as if she could read his thoughts again.

"Why did you throw that glass?" she asked.

Joel looked down and stared at his feet. He could see that his left foot was dirtier than his right one. It was always the same. And he didn't understand why. How could feet attract different amounts of muck?

"I don't know," he muttered. "I didn't mean to."

"Of course you meant to," she said. "Why else would you start throwing glasses around?"

Joel was still staring at his feet. He hadn't the slightest idea what to say. He couldn't possibly tell her that he suddenly found her revolting. That all he could see was the nose she didn't have on her face.

When he glanced up at her, he could see that her expression was very worried. A beam of light from the moon was illuminating her face. He had a guilty conscience.

"It was nothing," he mumbled.

Now he could look at her again. She looked him in the eye.

"I think you're growing up," she said.

That was something Joel was pleased to hear. That he was growing up. But there again, there was something in her tone of voice that worried him. What did she mean by saying that just now?

That was the kind of thing that grown-ups often did. Joel knew that he would have to learn—the most important thing was often not what was said.

But when it was said.

"There's nobody as childish as I am," he said.

She shook her head.

"You're growing up," she said again. "And before long, one of these days, you'll have forgotten that I exist. You might even fail to greet me when we meet in the street. Or you'll cross over to the other side."

Joel stared at her in astonishment.

"Why shouldn't I greet you?"

"Because you're embarrassed."

"What should I be embarrassed about?"

She replied by asking a question.

"Why did you throw that glass at the wall?"

If Joel had been holding a glass at that moment, he'd have hurled it at the wall. He wouldn't have cared less if he'd woken Samuel up.

Her questions made him angry. He was angry because she was right.

Even so, he shook his head.

"I didn't mean to," he said. "Why were you standing out there in the street? I might not have seen you."

"In that case I'd have thrown a snowball at your window. You've shown me before which is your bedroom window."

"That wouldn't have been a good idea," Joel said. "Samuel would have woken up. And he doesn't like me having girls in my room at this time of night."

If he could, he'd have bitten his tongue off. He could hear how stupid it sounded. Even if he hadn't even started playing forfeits yet. Now she would expose him for what he was.

But she didn't. She said nothing.

Instead she stood up so quickly that Joel gave a start.

"Anyway, now I know why you threw that glass at my kitchen wall," she said.

"But I haven't answered that question. All I've said is that I didn't mean to."

"That's enough for me," she said. "I'm going home now. And shouldn't you get some sleep?"

Joel tiptoed after her into the hall. Gertrud really knew how to move without making the slightest sound. He stood in the doorway and heard that she'd remembered which steps to avoid. She didn't leave a single creak behind.

He watched her from his window. Just like that dog, she materialized in the light from the streetlamp, then vanished. At that very moment he thought that she was less repulsive. At the same time, it seemed that something had changed forever that evening. But Joel couldn't work out what it was.

It was as if something was missing. Something that used to be there. But it had been replaced by something else. And he didn't know what it was.

He undressed and snuggled down into bed. He felt very tired.

He thought about Gertud, walking home through the night. She would have reached the railway bridge by now. But he had the feeling that somebody was coming towards her from the other direction. Somebody who passed Gertrud in the middle of the bridge. Somebody Gertrud hadn't noticed. At first he wasn't sure who it was. But then he knew. It was Ehnström's new shop assistant. And she was naked underneath transparent veils. Despite the fact that it was the middle of the night, and winter was nearly here, and it was freezing cold.

Joel gave a start. He had almost dreamt his way into slumber. He jumped out of bed and went to the window. But there was nobody there by the streetlamp. Certainly not a naked woman.

Joel went back to bed. Suppressed all thoughts about Gertrud.

Tomorrow he would find out who this new shop assistant was. She must have a name. She must live somewhere.

She must have her transparent veils hanging up on a coat hanger somewhere or other.

Perhaps on a coat hanger made of gold.

Needless to say, next morning Joel overslept. Samuel had to give him a good shaking and more or less lift him out of bed in order to wake him up.

"You'll be late for school if you don't get a move on."

"I'll manage."

He got washed and dressed, and sat down at the kitchen table with a glass of milk and a few sandwiches. He wasn't really hungry. But if he didn't eat now, he'd be hungry even before they'd finished singing the morning hymn.

"There's a funny smell in the kitchen," Samuel said out of the blue.

"Yes, it smells of herring," said Joel.

"No, it smells of perfume," said Samuel. "You'd almost be tempted to think there'd been a woman here last night, paying a secret visit."

Then he smiled. Joel could feel himself blushing. Had Samuel noticed that Gertrud had been here after all? Despite the fact that he'd been snoring all the time?

Joel waited anxiously for what was going to come next. Samuel could sometimes fly into a terrible temper. Often when you least expected it. But this time he just kept on smiling. And said nothing more. Just got ready for work, said goodbye and left.

Joel remained seated at the table. Gertrud always smelled of perfume. Joel was so used to it that he didn't even think about it.

What had Samuel meant? Had he noticed what had gone on?

Joel sat thinking about what would have been the right thing for him to say. He sat there so long that he was late for school, of course. Miss Nederström looked reproachfully at him when he entered the classroom. Otto was smirking, as usual. Joel hoped angrily that no woman would ever dance in transparent veils in front of *him*.

"If you go on like this I'll have to have a word with your dad," said Miss Nederström. "You arrive late far too often."

Joel said nothing, merely walked to his desk and sat down.

"Why are you late?"

"I overslept."

"Haven't you got an alarm clock?"

"It's broken."

"But surely your dad wakes you up?"

"He overslept as well."

The class giggled. Joel felt as if he'd painted himself into a corner. If he was asked just one more question, he would explode. This time he wouldn't merely throw a glass at the wall. This time he'd throw the whole world at Miss Nederström's face. But she didn't say anything more. The lesson continued.

It was math. And Joel kept getting his sums wrong. That was because he was spending all the time planning the expedition he would launch that same evening. When Ehnströms Livs closed, Joel would be lurking in the shadows, waiting for her.

He occasionally glanced at the Greyhound. She always got her sums right. He tried to get at least a third of the answers right by copying down what she had written.

On Wednesday evenings Samuel generally had dinner round at Sara's place. And then he would spend the night there. Sara was Samuel's girlfriend, and she worked at Ludde's bar in the center of town, just behind the Community Center. The atmosphere inside there was heavy with clouds of smoke, the smell of wet wool and old rubber boots. Early on, soon after Samuel had first met Sara, Joel had had problems with her. He'd been afraid she would take Samuel away from him. First of all Mummy Jenny had taken herself away from Joel. And now it looked like Sara was taking Samuel away as well.

But things were better now. Not least because Samuel seldom drank so much that he got drunk and started scrubbing the kitchen floor in the middle of the night. If there was anything Joel was afraid of, it was finding Samuel drunk. He was always worried about that possibility. Always prepared for the worst. But it hardly ever happened nowadays. And that had to be thanks to Sara.

The fact that it was Wednesday suited Joel down to the ground. He'd be able to sit at the kitchen table and work out his plans for the evening. He didn't need to prepare a proper dinner, but could get away with boiling a couple of eggs and making some sandwiches.

Ehnström's grocery shop closed at six. So he would have to be in place by then at the latest.

It was now a quarter past five. He'd need to leave in half an hour. He could feel the tension. Shadowing somebody who didn't know that you were there—that was about as good as it got for Joel.

A few years ago, he'd spent nearly all his time shadowing other people. He'd followed the vicar and the pharmacist, and even Stationmaster Knif. The only person he'd never tailed was Miss Nederström. But then, she never went out, apart from when she went to and fro between school and the house she lived in. Nobody had ever noticed Joel trailing them. He didn't know why following people was so exciting. Could it be because it meant that he was in charge of the situation? Time just flashed past.

Time for him to leave now. He laced up his boots and set off. At five minutes to six he was standing in the shadows on the opposite side of the street. He could see through the display window that there were still a few people in the shop. Then they left, one after another. The roller blind was pulled down inside the entrance door. *Closed.* Joel waited. Now he started to worry that she might not even be there tonight.

But then she emerged through the back door.

It was the new shop assistant, no doubt about it.

He waited until she had turned the corner by the furniture shop.

Then he started following her.

The adventure had begun.

— EIGHT —

Joel sneaked round the street corner.

There she was, up ahead. She'd crossed over the street and was walking along the opposite pavement. Joel waited until she had almost reached the derelict plot where the watchmaker's shop had been until it burnt down. Then he set off after her. She'd stopped at the kiosk. He couldn't see what she bought there. Joel was about to start following her again but he stopped dead. Samuel was coming towards him on the other side of the street. On his way to Sara's. Joel darted onto the derelict site and crouched down behind a pile of charred roof beams. He watched Samuel pass by. Now I'll never find her, he thought angrily. He hurried back into the street. There was nobody standing at the kiosk. He stopped at the window and took off one of his mittens. It was Old

Man Rudin who was serving. He was the one who used to sell Otto the magazines that weren't on display, but hidden away on a shelf under the counter.

"That woman who was here a couple of minutes ago dropped one of her mittens," Joel said.

"Leave it here," said Rudin. "No doubt she'll come back for it."

"But I want to have a word with her," said Joel. "Which direction did she go in?"

"I didn't see," said Rudin.

Joel left. There were three possible ways she could have gone. If he ran, he might just have a chance of seeing her. He picked the biggest street, the one leading to the church. And his luck was in. He caught a glimpse of her as she turned the corner by the old pharmacy.

He breathed a sigh of relief.

That had been close. You could always trust your parents to make a mess of things. Perhaps there were advantages in Mummy Jenny's disappearance after all. At the very least, he didn't have two problems to deal with. He had enough on his plate with Samuel.

She was heading for the buildings on the hill down to the river. So that was where she lived. Unless she lived out at Svensvallen, but that was several miles away. Or she might have a room at Rank's boardinghouse right on the edge of town. There were no other possibilities.

She stopped at the middle one of the three blocks of apartments, and went in through the front door. Joel kept his eye on the front of the building. After a couple of minutes a light went on in a second-floor window. So that was where she lived. Joel tried to work out what that implied. She might be lodging with somebody, but goodness only knows who. Or else she had her own apartment.

But as she hadn't rented a room in the boardinghouse, she must have come here to stay. She wasn't just working at Ehnström's shop for a couple of weeks.

Joel waited. He stamped his feet and jumped up and down so as not to be too cold. But his boots really were much too small for him. He'd have to have a word with Samuel, or his feet would be worn away.

Then he crossed the street and went in through the front door. He decided that if anybody came and asked what he was doing there, he would tell them he was looking for somebody called Sverker.

Just inside the front door was a board with the names of all the tenants. But there was a gap against one of the second-floor flats to the left. And that was where the light had gone on. Didn't she have a name? Or was it a secret? Joel decided it must be because she'd only just moved in. If there was a doorman or a caretaker or whatever, he wouldn't have had time to insert the name yet. Down at the bottom of the board was a row of unused letters for making the names by pressing them into the little holes on the surface of the board. Joel was very tempted to pick out some and press in a name: *Salome.*

But he didn't. Which was no doubt sensible of him. Instead he walked up the stairs. To make sure that nobody thought he was sneaking around, he trod down hard with his boots on each step. When he came to the second floor, he saw that there was a bit of paper with a name on the door to the left. He leaned forward in order to read it.

Mattsson, it said, written in red.

There was something else. In small letters, down at the bottom. The lighting was bad on the staircase. But he made it out in the end. It said: *Ehnström's Grocery Store.*

At that very moment the door opened. Joel gave a start and took a step backwards. Without his noticing, one of his bootlaces had come undone. He somehow stood on it, stumbled and fell to the floor.

It was her, all right, standing over him. But she wasn't wearing transparent veils. She had on a checked overall. And she was holding a sweeping brush.

"I thought you weren't going to come until tomorrow," she said, sounding surprised.

In the midst of his confusion it struck Joel that he'd been right: she certainly spoke with a Stockholm accent.

He scrambled to his feet. What the hell do I do now? he wondered. I hadn't planned for this.

"I said Thursday," she said. "It's only **Wednesday** today."

Joel tried to work out what on earth she was talking about. Was he supposed to have come tomorrow instead?

She suddenly burst out laughing. Joel stared at her red lips and white teeth.

"Why do you look so scared? And where's the catalog you were supposed to bring, with all the Christmas magazines?"

Sometimes, especially when he was in a corner, Joel had the ability to think quickly. He could sometimes surprise himself. He realized that she was mistaking him for somebody else. Somebody who was due to come the next day and show her a catalog with lots of Christmas magazines.

"I must have mixed up the day," Joel said.

"Where's the catalog?"

"It's downstairs."

Now he'd painted himself into a corner again. What if she asked him to fetch it? Then what would he do?

"Didn't Ehnström tell you my name?"

"I've forgotten it," he mumbled.

She looked at him and frowned.

"Ehnström said that Digby was sixteen. You can't be more than fourteen."

"Digby's my brother," said Joel.

"Your brother?"

"Digby's my brother, and he's ill."

"What's your name, then?"

"Joel."

"And you've come instead of him? But on the wrong day?"

"Digby had a fever and was rambling. He said Wednesday when he should have said Thursday."

"Is he very ill?"

"He's dislocated his knee."

"Does that give you a fever?"

"It can do up here in the north."

She shook her head.

"You'll have to come back tomorrow. I don't have time today."

"OK," said Joel. "I'll come back tomorrow."

She closed the door and was gone. Sweat was pouring off Joel. He retied his bootlace. He was about to start walking downstairs when he heard music coming from inside the flat. He pressed his ear to the door.

There was no mistake about it. It was Elvis Presley.

"Heartbreak Hotel."

Joel went down the stairs. But what he'd have preferred to do was to go back up, ring the doorbell and then embrace her when she answered. He felt all tingly at the very thought.

When he came out into the street, he turned to look up at her window. But she wasn't standing there looking at him.

He went straight home. The first tune he'd learn when Kringström had taught him to play the guitar was "Heartbreak Hotel."

It was echoing in his ears as he bounced home.

He had the delightful feeling that he'd turned into a

85

ball. Back there in her flat she was no doubt wandering around in transparent veils, listening to Elvis.

It was all too good to be true.

And Samuel was at Sara's. That was also good. Joel could be in peace. When he'd taken off his outdoor clothes and hurled his boots at the wall to punish them for being too small, he flopped down in Samuel's armchair and switched on the wireless. He put Samuel's pipe into his mouth and sucked at it. Pipe tobacco smelled good. But once, when he'd lit the pipe and inhaled the smoke, he'd felt sick. Lots of times he'd bought just one John Silver cigarette and tried smoking properly, but it tasted awful. He wondered what was wrong with him. Why couldn't he smoke like Otto, for instance? That would have to be one of his New Year's resolutions next year. To learn how to smoke properly.

He sucked at the empty pipe. The radio was playing classical music, Ludwig van Beethoven. But what Joel heard was "Heartbreak Hotel." "Heartbreak Hotel" with Elvis van Presley.

"Herbert's Hotel" with Joel van Gustafson.

What was going on? Ehnström had evidently arranged for somebody to visit her the next day to sell her some Christmas magazines. A boy. Unfortunately not Joel. But somebody by the name of Digby who from now on was Joel's elder brother. He didn't know how many boys in town were selling Christmas magazines, but there must be at least twenty of them. Most of them were around his age. He'd sold Christmas magazines himself last year, but this year he'd forgotten to tell the bookshop that he would be interested in doing it again. Somehow or other he'd have to borrow the catalog from whichever boy it was who was due to visit the new shop assistant.

Joel would wait there again tomorrow night. He'd have to think up a good excuse. And he'd have to raid his tin box, where he kept the money he'd saved. Always assuming there was anything left.

Joel put down the pipe and went to his room. He'd got the tin box from Samuel when he was a very little boy. Once upon a time it had contained cigars. It seemed to Joel that, after all those years, the smell of cigars still lingered. Nowadays he kept it under his bed. That was where he saved his money, when he had any. Which wasn't very often. He also used it to keep some attractive postage stamps from far distant lands that Samuel had visited when he was a sailor. He fetched the tin box and opened it. Just as he'd thought. Hardly any money left. Three kronor. He wasn't sure that would be enough to buy him the right to sell Christmas magazines to Ehnström's new shop assistant. That was a worry. But then it struck him that of course, he could opt not to make any money from selling any magazines to her. He could do the job for nothing.

He put the tin back under his bed. He felt sure that he'd solved the problem.

He went over to the window.

When it was dark it wasn't easy to see if it was cloudy or not. He went back to the kitchen and checked the thermometer outside the window. Plus one. Neither too warm nor too cold.

So, tonight was when he would start toughening up.

The person who was destined to sell Christmas magazines to a woman wearing transparent veils couldn't be just any Tom, Dick or Harry.

Samuel wasn't there, so he couldn't notice anything. If the alarm clock went off early enough, he could hide the bed away before Samuel got back home.

Joel hadn't yet made up his mind if he was going to tell Samuel about his plans to toughen himself up. There was a risk that his dad wouldn't understand, and would forbid him to sleep outside in the garden. But there again, Samuel was impressed by strength. He often talked about how strong he'd been as a young man. And about people he'd met who had achieved impressive feats of endurance. Perhaps Joel might be able to persuade Samuel to join him in sleeping out in the open now and then? Maybe that would do something towards correcting his dad's hunched back?

Joel sat down in Samuel's armchair. On the wireless, somebody was droning on and on about something or other. Joel tried to listen to what the man was saying in his squeaky voice. It had something to do with cows. Cows and milking machines. Joel started to fiddle with the tuning knob. Crackling sounds came from lots of different foreign stations, but sometimes he could hear a voice that was loud and clear. Occasionally he could hear music, and wondered what country it was coming from.

It was like traveling, he'd often thought. Without needing to get up from your armchair. You just twiddled a knob, and off you went.

He soon got tired of it all, and came back to the man talking about cows. He was still at it. Joel yawned. He had trouble keeping his eyes open. But it was still too early to go outside and go to bed.

He managed to keep awake until eleven o'clock. Then he put on several layers of clothes and packed his alarm clock into a wooly sock. Now he was ready. He was sure he'd fall asleep the moment he'd carried the bed out from the woodshed and snuggled down into it.

When he emerged into the garden, carrying his rolled-up mattress and all the bedclothes, it felt colder than he'd expected. No doubt that was because he was very tired. He opened the shed door and dragged out the bed. Some of the springs were broken, but that couldn't be helped. That could be a part of the toughening-up process.

He'd decided to place the bed behind the woodshed. Nobody would be able to see him there. But there again, it wasn't completely dark—the streetlamp penetrated that far.

He got everything ready, checked that the alarm clock stuffed into a sock was properly set, then crept down under the covers. He had his wooly hat on his head, and a woolen scarf wrapped round his face.

It felt cold when he'd settled down in bed. It was very odd, lying there and staring up at the night sky.

He could feel sleep creeping up on him. It felt less cold, now that he'd pulled the thick quilt over his head.

Before long he was fast asleep.

And the snow started to fall.

— NINE —

Joel dreamt that he was cold.

It was a strange dream. He was standing by the stove, stirring a saucepan. The stove was hot. So hot that he'd unbuttoned his shirt right down to his stomach so as not to sweat. But he was cold even so. He stirred and stirred, unfastened even more buttons, and sweat was pouring off him. But nevertheless, he was so cold that he was shivering.

Then he woke up. At first he didn't know where he was. It was his usual quilt that he'd pulled up over his head. But it was cold all around him. He tried to curl up even more. Then he noticed he was all stiff. And wet.

Then he remembered. He sat bolt upright.

The bed was almost entirely covered in snow. The brown quilt had a layer of fresh white snow. And the newly fallen snow had found its way into his bed and melted. He was so cold that he felt sick. He started to panic. Had he frozen to death? He jumped out of bed. His body was creaking. He started jumping up and down and flailing his arms about. Then he packed up the bedclothes and the wooly sock with the alarm clock. He left the bed where it was. He didn't bother about the creaking steps on the stairs. Once he was inside the flat he flung all the stuff he'd carried up with him into a heap on the floor, and sat down next to the radiator.

He couldn't remember ever having experienced anything so blissful.

The heat spread through his body. His hands softened up.

He fell asleep, sitting there by the radiator. He didn't know how long he slept. When he woke up he was still so tired that he could hardly open his eyes. Nevertheless, he forced himself to stand up, take off his boots and the rest of his clothes and put his pajamas on. He carried the mattress and the bedclothes into his room and put them on the bed. Everything was still wet. He took the alarm clock with him and snuggled down into Samuel's bed. It smelled of Samuel. It ought to have been the salty smell of the sea, but in fact it smelled of pine resin and forest.

He was woken up by somebody talking to him.

When he opened his eyes he found himself looking straight into Samuel's face.

This wasn't the first time Joel had slept in Samuel's

room when his dad had spent the night at Sara's place.

"Why is there a bed down there outside the shed?" Samuel asked.

"Is there?" said Joel.

"The shed door was open. I was going to close it when I noticed that old bed standing outside at the back. One of the corners was sticking out. It looked as if somebody had been sleeping there last night."

"Perhaps it was a tramp," said Joel.

Samuel frowned.

"Who sleeps out in the open when it's snowing? He'd have slept inside the shed, of course. Why lie outside and get covered in snow when it wasn't necessary?"

"Maybe it was somebody trying to toughen himself up."

The moment he said that, Joel realized he would never be able to tell Samuel what he was doing. He'd blown that possibility.

"It's very odd in any case," said Samuel. "Now you'd better hurry up or you'll be late for school."

Joel got up. His body felt as if it was made of iron. Before long he really would have to go to bed at the usual time. He couldn't remember ever feeling as exhausted as he did now.

He got washed and dressed. He took one look at his boots and was overcome by anger. He picked one of them up and marched out into the kitchen. Samuel was sitting at the table with his cup of coffee, humming a tune. He always hummed when he'd spent the night with Sara.

Samuel was not a good singer. Even his humming was out of tune. Joel wondered despondently if that meant that he, Joel, also sang out of tune.

You could bet your life that Elvis Presley's dad didn't sing out of tune.

"My boots are too small," he said. "I'm getting sores on my feet."

Samuel looked up from his coffee cup.

"Why's that?" he asked.

"I'm growing," said Joel. "My feet are getting bigger. I'll soon have to borrow your axe and cut holes in the boots for my toes."

Samuel nodded. That surprised Joel. His dad usually looked worried if they started talking about something that was going to cost money.

"Then you'll have to have a new pair, of course," he said. "We'll go to the shoe shop on Saturday."

Joel couldn't believe his ears. Had Samuel really understood what he'd said?

A new pair of boots would cost a lot of money.

Samuel started humming again as he put on his outdoor clothes.

Then he set off for work. It seemed to Joel that his dad's back wasn't quite as hunched as usual this morning.

He also realized that he'd discovered a secret. From now

on he would only ask for things that cost money after Samuel had spent the night with Sara. Never at any other time.

The feeling that Joel's body was as heavy as a fully loaded railway wagon had gone. Nothing could make Joel feel as energetic as he felt when Samuel had just agreed to pay for something that Joel wanted. He hurried to finish his breakfast, so as not to be late for school.

When school was over Joel was pleased to note that he hadn't fallen asleep during lessons a single time. I've already started to toughen up, he thought.

During the art class he'd also had time to think about what had happened the previous night. The mistake he'd made had been to decide to sleep in the open for a whole night right from the start. In future he'd start by aiming to sleep out just for an hour. When he woke up without feeling cold, he'd increase that to two hours. And then three. And so on, until he could cope with sleeping out of doors for a whole night. By then he'd be really tough.

As soon as school had finished Joel walked up the hill to Kringström's flat. This time he was happy to be accompanied by the Greyhound. He was sure that Kringström would make time to teach him to play the guitar. In which case, people's knowing about it had to be a good thing. As the Greyhound was more gossipy than most, it could be an idea to start by telling her. And before you could say Jack Robinson, the whole town would know.

He walked by her side up the hill.

"Where are you going?" she asked.

"I'm going to visit you," Joel said.

"Oh no, you're not."

"I'm going to sign your visitors' book."

"Oh no, you're not."

"I thought you might agree to get dressed up in transparent veils for me."

"Are you feeling all right? How childish can you get?"

"Yes, I'm childish, no doubt about it. Can you tell me what I should do in order not to be childish? So that I can be as grown-up as you are?"

"Go away and leave me in peace."

"Kringström's going to teach me how to play the guitar."

The Greyhound hesitated. Joel was pleased. She didn't know what to say.

"Is he really?"

"We're going to start today."

"But you can't play the guitar."

"I've just said, I'm going to learn."

"With hands like yours?"

"What do you mean? There's nothing wrong with my hands."

"You have to have long fingers. You don't."

Now it was Joel's turn to hesitate. He felt worried. Was she right? Did you really have to have long fingers? Were his fingers shorter than other people's?

The Greyhound grinned.

"You're telling porkies, Joel. You're making it up. You're not going to learn to play the guitar at all."

"You can go to hell."

"Go to hell yourself."

She grinned again, then started running. Joel knew there was no point in trying to catch up with her. She wasn't called the Greyhound for nothing. Miss Nederström used to say in PE lessons that the Greyhound was a prodigy. One of these days she was bound to become a Swedish running champion.

Or sprint champion, as Miss Nederström called it.

Ordinary people ran, but greyhounds and future gold medalists like Eva-Lisa sprinted.

But if he had been able to catch up with her he would have stuffed snow down her collar. Preferably down every item of clothing she was wearing.

When he came to the block of flats where Kringström lived he was still worrying about his fingers. How could you make them longer? Could you stretch them somehow or other? Or should you just let your fingernails grow longer?

Then he noticed, to his great disappointment, that Kringström's enormous van wasn't there.

Kringström's orchestra must have been playing at a dance somewhere or other.

He was just about to leave when one of the windows high up in the building opened. It was the Greyhound, of course. Even at that distance he could see that she was smirking.

"Kringström's gone to play at a dance," she said. "You'll have to find somebody else to teach you how to play the guitar."

"Where's he gone to?" Joel shouted.

"I'm not telling you," she shouted back. "But he's gone to Brunflo."

Joel knew that Brunflo was a town even further north. He didn't know if it was a big town or not, but just now the place annoyed him. He hoped that everybody living in Brunflo would soon move away. And that in the end there would be zero persons living there. Brunflo would be at the very bottom of the league table in *Where When How*. Kringström ought to have been at home, and placing a guitar in Joel's hands.

A guitar! Joel stopped dead.

He didn't have a guitar! And he hadn't seen one in Kringström's flat either. That was the only instrument Kringström didn't play, because everybody else did. And also because most of the ones who did play were involved in music that Kringström didn't approve of. Rock 'n' roll.

Joel trudged down the hill. How could he have been so stupid as to forget the most important thing of all? That he didn't have a guitar. All they had at home was a rusty old harmonica. Did he know anybody who had a guitar? Gertrud didn't, nor did any of his schoolmates he could consider asking. Some of them had accordions. And violins. A few had harmonicas. But nobody had a guitar.

He stopped dead. He'd seen a guitar somewhere or other. He was certain of it. The only question was where? Who had it? He started walking slowly, concentrating hard. He thought about all the homes he'd been in over the last few years. Ture had a guitar, but he'd taken it with him when he moved away. And Joel wouldn't have wanted to borrow that one anyway. He disliked Ture too much.

And then the penny dropped.

Simon Windstorm had a guitar. It was hanging on the wall in Simon's peculiar house in the trees. Joel didn't know if it was in good enough condition to play. He couldn't even remember if it had any strings. But it was a guitar. Deep chestnut brown in color. Almost black. Just like the record sleeve with Elvis Presley. When he sang "That's All Right, Mama." Or maybe it was "Hound Dog"?

He'd reached the bottom of the hill. From there he could see the hands on the church clock. It was too late to pay a visit to Simon Windstorm.

That would have to wait until tomorrow. Still, he was greatly relieved to have remembered somebody with a guitar. The Greyhound would start gossiping tomorrow. Joel would become a laughingstock if he didn't have a guitar.

Joel stood in the shadows and waited until the bus to Ånge had clattered past. Then he unbuttoned the four fly buttons on his pants. There should really have been five, but one had dropped off.

Then he started peeing and drew a yellow guitar in the snow. He had nearly enough for the whole thing, but when he came to the pegboard where you tightened the strings at the top of the neck, he had nothing left.

He stood and pulled at his willy for a while before fastening his fly. Thought about what he was going to do that evening. It was like scratching a mosquito bite. The same peculiar feeling.

He buttoned up his fly before it became completely stiff. Then he looked round guiltily. Had there been somebody in the shadows watching him?

He could hardly imagine anything more horrific. What if the Greyhound had seen what he was doing, for instance? He would have had to dig himself down in the churchyard next to Lars Olson. But without a stone telling everybody where he was buried.

By half past five he had prepared Samuel's meal and written a note that he left in the middle of the kitchen table.

I've already eaten. I've gone to the library. Joel.

He was in place outside the block of flats where she lived when she came home. She swayed slightly as she walked, the movement of her head tossing her hair about. When he put his hand in his pocket he could feel the money.

He started to worry again. What if it wasn't enough? He still didn't know who would come. His supposed brother called Digby, who was sixteen years old.

He waited. Tried to think about the boots he was going to buy with Samuel. But all the time he could see veils hanging in front of him. Veils that he couldn't yet quite see through.

Six o'clock came, then half past six. He was starting to feel cold now. He decided he wouldn't do any toughening up that night. Not even for an hour. Besides, he had a whole year ahead of him. If he only toughened up every third night, that would still be more than a hundred times before the year was out. Then he tried to work out how many days, weeks and months would pass by before the year 2045. How many had gone already, and how many did he have left? He kept losing count and having to start all over again.

And then he saw a boy walking towards the building. He was carrying something under his arm. Joel knew immediately that it was Digby. But he couldn't yet make out who it was.

Now the boy was approaching a streetlamp.

Joel couldn't believe his eyes.

Otto!

Otto was the last person he wanted to talk to. But he couldn't get out of it now.

Otto had already seen him.

So he was the one selling the Christmas magazines. Of all the people in existence, it had to be Otto, of course.

Joel felt like screaming out loud in anger. But he didn't. What he did do was to step forward and stand in Otto's way.

There's going to be a duel, he thought.

A duel over a Christmas magazine catalog.

— TEN —

Otto peered suspiciously at Joel.

Joel tried to peer threateningly back at him. The catalog Otto was carrying under his arm was for Christmas magazines. There was no doubt about that.

So Otto was Digby.

Digby, Piggy, Pigmy. Of course it would have to be him. It was bound to be him.

"What are you doing here?" asked Otto.

Joel didn't like his tone of voice. It was shrill. And Otto was speaking too loudly.

"I want to talk to you," said Joel.

"Talk, then!"

"I am."

Silence. Otto was still peering at him. Joel got ready to defend himself.

"You've got something I want to buy," he said.

Otto's curiosity was instantly aroused. He had nothing against earning a bit of money by doing a deal. He took a step closer to Joel.

"What?"

"The woman you're going to sell Christmas magazines to in this block of flats is a relative of mine," Joel said. "I thought I might give her a surprise."

Otto became suspicious again.

"But she's from Stockholm. You haven't got any relatives there, surely?"

Joel was ready for that.

"She's a cousin of my dad's stepbrother."

Otto hesitated. Joel's reply had been quick and firm. And in addition, a cousin of a father's stepbrother was sufficiently complicated to make it impossible to work out on the spot what it really meant. It could just as easily be true as not.

"Surely you know what a cousin of a stepbrother is?" said Joel.

"Of course I do."

"I thought you might let me sell her the Christmas magazines. You'd still get all the money she'll pay for them. Plus three kronor in cash."

"I want five," said Otto promptly.

Joel knew now he was going to be successful. Otto didn't care about Christmas magazines or cousins or stepbrothers anymore. He was interested in the money. Nothing else.

"Five is too much. Besides, you know I'm good at selling Christmas magazines. I'll sell at least one more than you would have done."

Otto said nothing. Last year Joel had sold more Christmas magazines than almost everybody else in town. Otto knew that what Joel said was true.

"I want five," he said again.

"You'll get three," said Joel. "Tomorrow."

"I want the money now."

"Tomorrow."

"Now."

Joel pretended to think it over.

"Tomorrow," he said again.

"Now."

It was crunch time.

"Give me the catalog. I'll give you three kronor."

"Now."

"Yes. Now."

Otto handed over the catalog. Joel handed over the three coins. The duel was over. Joel had defeated his opponent. He could put his invisible pistol back into its holster.

"It'll probably take quite a while," said Joel. "I'll return the catalog at school tomorrow."

Otto became suspicious again.

"You're not thinking of selling to anybody else as well, I hope?"

"No, only to my cousin."

"But you said she was the cousin of your father's stepbrother."

"That means she's my cousin as well. Don't you know anything?"

Otto didn't answer. That's one way in which he and I are alike, Joel thought. Neither of us likes being wrong.

Joel had got the catalog. Otto had put the money in his pocket.

"There's something fishy about this," he said. "Why should you want to give me three kronor, just so that you can surprise your cousin?"

"I got the money from my dad," said Joel. "He's the one who wants me to surprise her."

Joel knew that if you said something that wasn't really true, it had to be nearly true. Otherwise nobody would believe anything you said.

"I want the catalog back tomorrow morning," said Otto. "And if you don't sell her any magazines, I want three more kronor."

"I'll sell some all right," said Joel.

Otto walked away. Joel breathed a sigh of relief. It hadn't been easy, but he'd succeeded.

He went in through the front door and up the stairs. When he came to her door, he ran his hand over his hair, making sure it was standing straight up. Joel had a crew cut, and it was important that his hair stand straight up. The only problem was that he had a cowlick right at the front, over his forehead. There, his hair spread out like a fan. Samuel didn't have a cowlick like that, so he must have inherited it from his mum, Jenny.

A fan over his forehead.

There were a few moments in life when Joel was glad that Mummy Jenny had disappeared. There were a few things he'd like to give her a piece of his mind about.

He was feeling nervous. He wondered if this Mattsson woman was another one like Gertrud, who could read his thoughts. What if, when she opened the door, she was wearing transparent veils with nothing on underneath? What would he do then? Pretend he hadn't noticed? Go into her flat, ask her to leaf through the catalog and choose whatever magazines she wanted to order? Or would he do what Samuel used to say?

"Soon you'll be old enough to start taking the girls in your arms."

What did he mean by that? Should Joel lift her up?

Samuel was never any good at explaining what he meant.

It got even more difficult when Joel thought of what else Samuel used to say.

"Make sure they don't get pregnant. You'll be arrested if they do."

Sometimes Joel had the feeling that he knew how it all happened. But deep down he had a nagging worry that he didn't really know anything at all. Then he would be afraid that everybody else, and especially Otto, knew all about what he ought to know. But there were other times when he suspected that Otto knew just as little as he did. Otto was all talk. He still hadn't grasped why human beings had two ears but only one tongue.

It was because they should listen more and speak less.

Joel kept on stroking away at his hair. But he couldn't wait any longer. He would have to take a step out into the unknown. It was just too bad that, needless to say, he badly needed a pee.

He rang the bell. There was no music to be heard from inside the flat this time.

The door opened, and there she was before his very eyes.

Salome Mattsson.

But she was not covered in transparent veils. She was wearing long trousers and a striped blouse.

"At least you're punctual," she said.

She let him into the hall. Joel felt lost and didn't know what to do next. Was it here in the hall that he was supposed to lift her up? Or should he ask her to put her veils on?

"Take your boots off," she said. "You'll make a mess of my clean floor if you don't."

Joel sat down on a little stool and started undoing his

laces. When he took off his left boot he saw that he had a big hole in his woolen sock.

I'd better leave, he thought. I can't let her see me with holes in my socks.

"What's keeping you?" she shouted from inside the living room. "There's a program I want to listen to on the radio starting soon."

Joel removed the other boot as fast as he could, and tried to fold the hole in his sock underneath his foot. When he walked he looked as if he were limping. He ran his hand one last time through his hair. Then he went into the living room. She was sitting in an armchair with her legs tucked underneath her, smoking. Joel could smell perfume, but not the one that Gertrud used. There wasn't a lot of furniture in the flat. She gave him a smile. Not friendly, but not unfriendly either.

"How long are you going to stand there looking like a fish out of water? Let me have the catalog while you're wondering where to sit. What was your name again?"

"Joel," said Joel.

"How's Digby?"

"He still has a high temperature, but his shoulder's not so painful."

She looked at him in surprise.

"I thought you said it was his knee that hurt?"

"His knee and his shoulder as well," said Joel quickly.

She shook her head and started looking through the

catalog. Joel sat down on the edge of a chair. He really did need to go for a pee now.

She leafed through the catalog. Joel sat watching her. She certainly was very beautiful.

Even before she'd got halfway through, he'd made up his mind that this was the woman he was going to marry.

"Which one of these is really good?" she asked.

Joel hadn't even had time to open the catalog, never mind read it. He tried to think back to the year when he'd sold Christmas magazines.

"Maybe *The Girls' Own Christmas Book*," he suggested tentatively.

She snorted.

"That's for little kids."

Joel had nothing else to suggest. He waited, unable to take his eyes off her. Now he so needed a pee that he had to cross his legs and press as hard as he could.

"You've got a hole in your sock," she said out of the blue.

Damn, Joel thought. She's noticed.

"You'd better tell your mum to mend it for you," she said.

"I will," said Joel.

She closed the catalog and yawned.

"I'll take a copy of *The Family Christmas Magazine*," she said. "Klara can have it as a Christmas present."

Joel reached out to take the catalog, and produced a pencil.

"So, I'll have to make a note of the name," he said.

"Klara Ehnström."

Joel was confused.

"If it's you who's placing the order, yours is the name I have to make a note of," he said.

"Sonja Mattsson," she said. "Svensvallsvägen 19. Will that do?"

"That'll be fine."

So she wasn't called Salome. But Sonja wasn't all that different. It started with the same letter.

Joel was feeling less nervous now. If only he didn't need a pee so urgently.

"Are you from Stockholm?" he asked.

"I hope you can hear that from the way I speak," she said.

"Have you moved here, then?"

"I needed to get away for a while. And the Ehnströms are relations of ours. But I don't know how long I'll stay here. It depends."

"Depends on what?"

She had lit another cigarette.

"You're a real Nosey Parker, aren't you?"

Joel blushed. He felt as if he was going to wet his pants at any moment. If he didn't leave this very second, there could be a catastrophe.

"I have to go now," he said, standing up. "Do you like Elvis?"

"Is there anybody who doesn't?"

"I've thought about becoming a rock idol," said Joel. "I've just started practicing."

She burst out laughing. Joel couldn't work out if it was malicious or not.

"Then you'll have to come and perform for me," she said.

"Yes," said Joel. "When I've finished practicing."

Then he rushed out into the hall and started pulling on his boots. He couldn't keep control of his bladder for much longer. She was standing in the doorway to the living room, watching him.

As he was putting on his jacket, Joel noticed that one of his mittens was in danger of falling out of his pocket. That gave him an idea. She had withdrawn into the living room in order to stub out her cigarette. Joel took out the mitten and hid it behind some wooly hats lying on the shelf. Now he had an excuse to come back again. And when he did, he would make sure he didn't need a pee.

"Pass on greetings to Digby," she said. "I hope he's soon better."

"He will be, don't worry," said Joel.

He opened the door. Then he turned round.

"I'd like to learn how to speak with a Stockholm accent," he said.

"You wouldn't be able to do that," she said.

"I can do anything," said Joel. Then he closed the door and raced down the stairs with the catalog in his hand.

He came out into the street and pressed himself close to the wall.

There were times when having a pee was the most satisfactory thing in life.

Then he headed for home. He was already looking forward to the next day. He noticed that he was bouncing like a ball again. It didn't matter anymore that his boots were too small. He would buy some new ones. And when he went back Sonja Mattsson would be sitting in her armchair, smoking. When he sang and played for her the first time, she would start screaming and pulling at his clothes.

He tried to think of the last time he'd been in such a good mood as this. But he couldn't remember.

He cleared the staircase in three almighty jumps, and barged in through the door. Samuel would be sitting there next to the wireless, and Joel would sit down beside him. He wouldn't say a word about Sonja Mattsson. Nor would he mention the fact that he'd started toughening himself up and had decided to become a rock idol.

All he wanted was for Samuel to see what a really happy person looked like.

That was something he could do with, after a long, strenuous day out in the forest.

But Joel stopped dead when he came to the kitchen.

Samuel wasn't at home.

He felt as if he'd been punched in the stomach.

Samuel was always at home, except on Wednesdays, when he stopped over at Sara's.

Samuel was always at home. Unless...

Joel didn't have the strength to follow that thought through.

If Samuel wasn't at home, he must be drinking. If he was drinking, he could turn up at any time of day or night.

Joel shuddered at the thought. Surely Samuel hadn't started drinking again? Everything had been going so well ever since he'd met Sara.

His fear changed into anger. This simply couldn't be the case, surely?

He checked Samuel's bedroom. Nobody asleep in the bed.

What Joel wanted to do most of all was to cry. That confounded Samuel always spoiled everything when Joel was feeling happy.

Joel put his wooly hat back on and trudged down the stairs. He paid no attention to all the creaking.

He emerged into the empty streets and started looking for Samuel. It was like looking for a ship that had been stranded on a deserted beach. When Samuel had been drinking, he was like a shipwrecked sailor.

Joel didn't need to search for long. On the hill leading up to the station he saw a shadowy figure staggering towards him. It was Samuel, who was barely capable of standing up.

Joel ran towards him. He caught up with him underneath a streetlamp. Samuel's eyes were bloodshot.

He was drunk.

But Joel noticed something else.

Samuel was devastated.

Something must have happened.

"You've come to meet me, have you?" said Samuel, his voice slurred.

"Yes," said Joel. "Let's go home now."

He supported Samuel and led him along the street.

He had found his shipwrecked father.

— ELEVEN —

Joel made some coffee.

He hated everything to do with strong drink, especially the Swedish version of spiced vodka, called _bränn-
vin_. He had no need to make any New Year's resolutions
concerning _brännvin_: he would never start drinking it. It
was enough to see what it did to Samuel.

Joel used to find bottles hidden away all over the
house, labeled "Absolutely pure _brännvin_." He found
them hidden in the firewood bin, and in the case of ap-
ples they had tucked away in the pantry, for eating in the
winter. He'd even found a bottle once in the cupboard
where they kept sheets and pillowcases.

He'd read somewhere that the great Indian chieftain
Geronimo used to call _brännvin_ "firewater," but Joel
knew what it really was.

Spirits turned Samuel into a shipwrecked sailor.

The drink took the boat away from a sailor.

And Samuel was and would always be a sailor, even though he worked in the forests nowadays, chopping down trees.

Joel made the coffee very strong. He knew that would help to sober Samuel up. Meanwhile, Samuel was lolling about at the kitchen table. He must have fallen down in the street somewhere. One of his pants legs was wet and dirty. Joel didn't want to ask where his dad had been. When Samuel was on a drinking spree he would go to the homes of other men in town who spent all their time being washed up like driftwood on a beach, like shipwrecked sailors.

Joel still had a stomachache, but it felt better now that he'd found Samuel. His biggest fear was always that Samuel would fall into a snowdrift one of these days and doze off to sleep.

Despite the amount of spirits that Samuel had drunk over the years, he had never learnt how to cope with it.

Joel wanted to know what had happened. Why had Samuel started drinking just now? When he'd been keeping off the booze for so long?

But first Samuel must drink his coffee. Joel poured out a cup and put it on the table in front of his father. He'd put three sugar lumps in it.

Samuel's eyes were very red. Joel sat down at the table opposite him. It was the spirits glowing red in Samuel's eyes. The firewater had burnt, and all that was left of it was a glow deep down in Samuel's eyes.

"I'm very sorry about this," said Samuel.

"So am I," said Joel testily.

Samuel slurped at his coffee. He was holding the cup in both hands. Joel waited until he'd put it down again.

"What's the matter?" he asked.

"Nothing," said Samuel.

Joel didn't ask anymore. He knew that Samuel would tell him what had happened sooner or later. It might be soon, or it might take time. But sooner or later, when the spirits had begun to leave his body, he would say what was wrong.

Meanwhile Joel sat at the table, daydreaming. He thought about Sonja Mattsson and the way she sat with her legs tucked underneath her. If he didn't have Samuel to run around after and take responsibility for, he could move in with her. He would be able to practice there on the guitar he hoped to borrow from Simon Windstorm. Her flat smelled of perfume, not of wet wool.

"It's Sara," Samuel said all of a sudden.

"What's the matter with Sara?"

"She doesn't want to anymore."

Joel still didn't understand what had happened. Samuel raised his head, which seemed to be attached very loosely to his body. Like a leaf clinging to a tree in autumn. A leaf that was about to fall off.

"She met me when I came home from the forest," said

Samuel. "And she said she'd been thinking. And that it was probably best if we stopped seeing each other."

So she's broken it off, Joel thought.

That was the explanation. But he still didn't understand. Samuel had always said how well they got on together. How they laughed a lot. And he spent the night with her once a week.

"Didn't she explain why?" Joel asked.

Samuel shook his head. He'll start crying in a minute, Joel thought.

At that very moment Samuel burst out crying. It cut through Joel like a knife. This was the worst and the most difficult thing. Samuel drifting ashore like a shipwrecked sailor was one thing. But when he started crying, it was like having to deal with a drowning man.

What Joel wanted to do more than anything else was to start crying himself. But he didn't, of course. He stood up and walked round the table. Patted Samuel on the head.

When Samuel cried, it sounded as if he was squeaking. He was trying to say something, but the words jumped out of his mouth in a chaotic jumble. Joel gathered he was trying to explain why Sara wanted to break off the relationship, but he couldn't understand what his father was saying.

Afterwards everything was very silent.

Samuel sat staring at his coffee cup. It occurred to Joel that Sara had now done the same as Mummy Jenny. She'd deserted Samuel.

"Has she gone away?" Joel asked. "Did she also pack a bag and vanish?"

"She's still here," Samuel said. "Why should she want to leave here? It's only me she doesn't want to see anymore."

Joel helped Samuel to go to bed. Took off his shoes and pulled a blanket over him. Then he sat in the kitchen and waited until he was sure that Samuel really had fallen asleep. By this time Joel was so tired that he didn't bother to get undressed either, but just lay down on top of the bed. Pulled the quilt over his head. Listened to Samuel's snores rumbling in through the wall.

When Joel woke up next morning he jumped out of bed and went to check if Samuel was still there. To make sure his father hadn't woken up and sneaked out to find something else to drink. But to Joel's surprise Samuel was sitting at the kitchen table. He was eating breakfast and had already made up his lunch box.

He looked guiltily at Joel.

"That wasn't good, what happened yesterday," he said. "But it won't happen again."

Joel knew that might be true, but there again, it might not. Samuel had said the same thing so many times before.

"What's happened?" Joel asked.

"It's all over between Sara and me," said Samuel. "It came as a complete surprise."

Joel didn't ask any more. He could see that Samuel would start crying again if he did.

"You'd better get a move on or you'll be late for school," Samuel said, getting to his feet.

Joel watched him trudging off towards the forest, shoulders hunched.

Joel had no intention of going to school. He didn't have the strength.

It was all this business with Sara. What had really happened? One day everything seemed to be fine. The next day Samuel came rolling home with his eyes red from all the firewater.

Joel made up his mind on the spot. He must find out the truth. He got dressed and left the house. There was always a risk that somebody would catch him. Realize that he was playing truant. But he would have to do what he'd made up his mind to do. It was too early for Sara to be at work in Ludde's bar. She would still be at home.

When he knocked on the door of Sara's flat, she answered the door almost immediately. She was in her dressing gown and had rollers in her hair.

She smiled in surprise when she saw Joel.

That made him angry. Samuel had sat at the kitchen table, crying. Sara stood there smiling. That wasn't fair.

"Joel!" she said. "This is a surprise. Aren't you at school?"

She let him in. Joel purposely didn't wipe his feet and

hoped he would bring in lots of dirt to make a mess of the floor.

He realized now just how much he disliked Sara. He could remember what it had been like right at the beginning, when Sara and Samuel first started seeing each other. That feeling came back now. What he wanted to do more than anything else was to hit her.

They went to her kitchen.

"I assume you've come to ask what happened," she said.

At last she was looking serious.

Joel nodded, but he didn't say anything.

"I like your dad very much," she said. "But we don't really suit each other."

"It's you who don't suit him," said Joel. "There's nothing wrong with Samuel."

"I didn't say there was."

"Then why don't you suit each other?"

"Perhaps we don't really want the same things."

The only thing that's good about Sara, Joel thought, is that she talks to me as if I were grown up.

Joel decided to speak his mind.

"You don't know what's best for you," he said. "You'll never find anybody better than Samuel."

She wasn't angry. She just sat looking at him.

"Did you know that Samuel wanted us to get married?" she asked.

Joel's heart stopped beating. That couldn't be true. But that was what she said. And Sara didn't usually tell lies.

"I gather that you didn't know," she said after a while. "But when Samuel popped the question I needed to make up my mind. And I don't want to get married. If there's one who wants to get married and another who doesn't, they can't very well carry on seeing each other."

Joel was stumped. Had Samuel really thought about marrying Sara? Without discussing it with him first?

Joel didn't feel sorry for Samuel anymore. Now he was just angry. And disappointed. Samuel had gone behind his back. Maybe Samuel had even intended to run off with Sara and leave Joel behind.

"What are you thinking about?" Sara asked.

"Nothing," said Joel. "I'd better be going now."

"You mustn't think that I find this easy," she said as they stood in the hall.

She patted Joel on the cheek. Joel couldn't make up his mind if he liked that, or if he ought to hit her.

He left. Looked around. No sign of any of the teachers who would see that he was playing truant.

It was cold. He missed the mitten that was hidden in Sonja Mattsson's flat. He checked the church clock and saw that it was still early. A quarter past eight. He wondered if he ought to call on Gertrud. But he didn't feel like talking to her either. So there was only one person left.

He started walking up the hill towards the hospital. Past there, beyond the edge of the little town, was Simon Windstorm's house. As Joel had no intention of going to school, he could go there and ask if he could borrow the guitar.

Joel had met Simon Windstorm when he'd been looking for that remarkable dog that was heading for a distant star. Simon used to drive around at night like a lost soul in his old truck, when he couldn't sleep.

Simon Windstorm wasn't all there. Everybody knew that. He was so mad that he'd spent a long time locked away in a mental hospital. But Joel knew he wasn't really mad. In fact it sometimes seemed to Joel that he was the only person who had realized that Simon was cleverer than anybody else around.

Simon Windstorm had taken Joel to Four Winds Lake. There he'd taught Joel how to listen in a way he'd never been able to do before.

The winds had voices. The breeze had a language of its own.

He thought about that as he passed by the hospital, and soon he'd left the last houses in the town behind him. He was walking fast because he was cold. Then he turned off the main road and followed the path to Simon's cottage. The truck was parked outside. As usual the courtyard was full of junk, half buried in the snow. A hen that must have been suffering in the cold was wandering around, pecking away. Joel stood still and listened. There was a swishing sound in the trees. Smoke was belching out of the chimney. So Simon was at home. He was probably reading one of the many books he owned, rewriting the closing pages so that it all ended up as he wanted it to do.

Joel went up to the door and knocked. Simon never invited anybody to come in. So Joel opened it and entered. Simon was sitting by the open fire, wrapped up in an old bearskin. Two dogs were lying at his feet. They wagged their tails when they saw Joel. Simon screwed up his ageing eyes.

"I had a dream about you last night," he said. "Joel Gustafson, the great conqueror. And now, here you are."

Joel had noticed straightaway that the guitar was hanging on the wall. He went to take a closer look at it. It had four strings; two were missing. But there was no doubt that it could be played.

"I've come to ask if I can borrow your guitar," Joel said. "I promise to look after it well."

Simon put his book down on his knee.

"Of course you can borrow it," he said. "Are you going to join the Salvation Army?"

"I've decided to become a rock singer."

"Hm. I don't really know what that is," said Simon.

"A rock idol? Like Elvis?"

"I go in for old bearskins myself."

It was obvious to Joel that Simon had no idea what a rock singer was. No doubt he'd never heard of Elvis either. Simon was old and peculiar. It wasn't his fault that he didn't know what was going on in the world.

Joel carefully unhooked the guitar from the wall.

"There's an old case somewhere," said Simon thoughtfully. "But I haven't a clue where."

"I'll look for it," said Joel. "I've got all day."

That was just as well. It took many hours of searching before he found the moth-eaten old guitar case hidden away in one of Simon's outhouses. When he went back in, he found Simon asleep in his chair. Joel didn't want to wake him up. He knew that Simon had spent all his life finding it difficult to fall asleep.

The dogs wagged their tails as Joel sneaked out through the front door.

They were standing guard over Simon's sleep.

Joel spent the rest of the day at home, trying to work out how the guitar functioned. He plucked at the strings and pretended that he could play. But all the time he was thinking about Samuel. And about what Sara had said.

He prepared dinner in good time. He laid the table with a clean cloth, so that Samuel would feel he was eating just as elegantly as he would have done at Sara's place. Samuel would regret ever having asked her to marry him.

Joel could see that something good might come out of what had happened. Maybe Samuel might start thinking now about his own best interests.

They could leave this godforsaken place. The sea was waiting for them.

Joel stood in the window, looking out for Samuel. It was dark already. He'd appear at any moment. But all the time Joel could feel a worry gnawing away inside him. Had his dad gone out drinking again? You never knew with Samuel.

What Joel really wanted to do was to call on Sonja Mattsson and collect his mitten. When she opened the door today, perhaps she'd be dressed in transparent veils?

Joel sighed. It wasn't possible.

He'd always been his own mum. Now he would have to be dad to his own father.

He gazed out the window. Waited for Samuel.

Waited and waited.

And the food got cold.

— TWELVE —

Joel woke up with a start.

He had dozed off at the kitchen table while he'd been waiting for Samuel. He didn't know what time it was. But he could hear footsteps on the stairs. It could only be Samuel. He stood up. Would Samuel be sober or not?

The door opened. Joel felt himself sinking down into his relief like getting into a warm bath. Samuel's eyes were not red. He wasn't swaying from side to side. He was late home, but he hadn't been drinking.

"Are you still up?" he asked in surprise.

Joel wondered how stupid Samuel could get. Did he really think Joel would have gone to bed and fallen asleep before Samuel came home? He felt the need to make that clear.

"How could I possibly go to bed when you were out on a spree?"

"It depends what you mean by on a spree," said Samuel. "I've been at Sara's place, trying to talk some sense into her."

Joel waited eagerly for what came next, but Samuel didn't say anything more. Joel wondered, a bit uncomfortably, if Sara had said anything about his going there as well. He didn't know how Samuel would react. He didn't usually like it if anybody stuck their nose into his business. That was one of the things he and Joel had in common.

Samuel hung up his jacket and kicked off his boots.

"What time is it?" Joel wondered.

"It must be turned midnight," said Samuel. "We'd both better get to bed if we're going to be able to cope with tomorrow."

Samuel seemed less miserable than yesterday.

"How did it go?" Joel asked tentatively.

Samuel shrugged.

"She thinks we're not suitable for each other," he said. "Maybe she's right. But I don't understand why."

Joel said nothing. Sara had evidently not mentioned that he'd been to see her. If she had, Samuel would have said so by now. Joel had got away with it.

"We didn't sit shouting at each other," said Samuel. "I had dinner, and we spoke calmly and sensibly. But I suppose that's that. We're on our own again, you and me."

That's how it's been all the time, Joel thought. You've had Sara to go home to. I haven't.

Samuel yawned.

"We can talk more about this tomorrow," he said. "We'd better get to bed now. We can have the food you've prepared for tomorrow's dinner."

They carried the pots and pans to the pantry; then Joel had a quick wash and snuggled down into bed.

Anyway, it was a relief. That Samuel wasn't drunk again. There was nothing worse than that. Nothing at all.

When Joel arrived at school the next day he had a nasty surprise. Somebody had seen him in the street the previous day. Miss Nederström called him out to the front after they'd sung the morning hymn.

"Why weren't you at school yesterday?" she asked sternly.

"I was ill," said Joel.

She turned white in the face with anger.

"How dare you stand there telling me barefaced lies?" she thundered. "The headmaster saw you at the kiosk yesterday morning."

Joel wondered whether to say he'd been to the doctor's, but he didn't. It would be too easy to check that. So he said nothing, just stared down at the floor. Behind him the rest of the class was sitting in tense silence. He couldn't see them, but he knew that was the case. And that Otto would be smirking.

"You were playing truant," said Miss Nederström. "And it's not the first time."

Joel continued staring at the floor.

"Have you nothing to say?"

What could he say? Nobody would understand. Least of all Miss Nederström. He continued to say nothing.

"You can stay in after school today," said Miss Nederström. "Go and sit down."

Joel walked back to his desk. He tried to avoid looking at Otto. He couldn't bear the thought of seeing that smirk of his.

Still, he was glad he'd remembered to bring the Christmas magazine catalog. He wondered how much Otto would demand for returning it a day late.

He found out during the first break. Otto came storming towards him.

"I want three kronor more," he said. "You were supposed to return the catalog yesterday."

Joel handed it over.

"I sold a magazine to my dad's cousin," he said. "And I was ill."

Otto looked as if he was going to hit him.

"You were playing truant," he said. "You weren't ill. And I want three kronor."

Something snapped inside Joel. All that business with Samuel had been too much for him. And all the other things he was worrying about.

He hurled himself at Otto, as if he were trying to force open a door that had stuck. They both fell to the ground. Immediately a ring of spectators formed round them. And then they started fighting. Otto was the stronger, but Joel was so furious that he found himself with strength he didn't really possess.

They only stopped fighting when the headmaster and Miss Nederström managed to separate them.

Both Joel and Otto received a box on the ear from the headmaster. It was a hard blow and really hurt.

The headmaster glared at Joel.

"Not only do you play truant," he said, "but when you come back to school you start fighting."

"He started it," said Otto.

Joel said nothing. He didn't feel angry anymore. He just felt tired now.

What he would really have liked to do was to go away. Leave school behind and never come back.

But the outcome was that both Joel and Otto had to stay in after school. Otto for an hour, Joel for two. As they were both bad at handwriting, they had to spend the time practicing.

Otto left after an hour.

Miss Nederström sat at her desk reading a magazine. And Joel practiced his writing. But he couldn't make the letters look neat.

Eventually she looked at the clock and closed her magazine.

"You can go now," she said. "But come here first."

Joel did as he was told.

"I don't think you would play truant unless there was a reason," she said. "Are you still going to refuse to tell me why you did it?"

He would have liked to. Explain what he felt like when Samuel came home drunk. But he said nothing. He couldn't.

Miss Nederström sighed and shook her head.

"I can't make you out," she said. "But you can go now."

Joel went. He ought really to have collected the guitar and gone to Kringström's flat. But he didn't feel up to it. He was tired and miserable. He felt lonely and he felt worn out. Life was hard and his boots were too small for him. He went down to the river and walked along the path that followed the riverbank. Paused by the rocks where he used to play a lot a few years back. He hardly ever went there nowadays. He suddenly felt a desire to go back to that time. Life had been hard when he was eleven as well, but in a different way.

It wasn't as easy to enter a dreamworld now. If he stood staring into the river now he didn't see any crocodiles. Only logs floating down to the sawmill at the river mouth.

That was in fact the most difficult bit. Not being able to see crocodiles anymore. Only logs.

When he got home he started warming up the food he'd prepared yesterday. As he did so, he made up his mind to go round to Sonja Mattsson's that evening and collect his mitten.

He had another worry as well. How would he be able to lie out in the open and toughen himself up if Samuel stopped spending the night at Sara's every Wednesday? That was a problem. Perhaps Samuel would find somebody else? In any case, there were three more waitresses at Ludde's bar.

Samuel came home and he was sober. They had dinner.

"How did it go at school today?" he asked.

"We had a lot of handwriting practice," said Joel.

Samuel didn't normally ask more than one question about school. He didn't today either. And Joel was grateful for that.

When Joel started getting ready to go out, Samuel looked up from his newspaper.

"You didn't get much sleep last night," he said. "You must go to bed early tonight."

"I'm only going to fetch a mitten I lost the other day."

"Where?"

"I left it behind at somebody's house."

"Whose?"

"A friend's."

Samuel nodded.

"In case I'm asleep when you come home, I'd better say good night now."

"I won't be late."

When Joel started walking down the street and his boots began chafing against his ankles, he tried to imagine that he was walking along a beach. With palm trees. And it was warm. He searched through his mind for the shipwrecked Captain Joel Gustafson. But he couldn't find him.

When he came to the building where Sonja Mattsson lived, he paused outside the door and made sure he didn't need a pee. That was the most important thing of all. Then he took off his wooly hat and ran his hand through his short-cropped hair.

He felt nervous. He hoped something was going to happen. But he didn't know what.

He went up the stairs and rang the doorbell. When she opened the door she was wearing the same clothes as last time. Still no transparent veils.

"What do you want?" she asked. "Don't think I'm going to buy any more Christmas magazines."

"I've lost a mitten and I think I must have left it here," said Joel.

Now came the hard bit. There was a risk that she might leave him waiting at the door while she went to look for the mitten.

"Come in," she said. "It's so cold with the door open."

She closed the door behind him. Joel breathed in her perfume. If he'd dared, he would have grabbed hold of her and lifted her up.

"Have a look, then," she said. "See if the mitten's lying here somewhere."

She left him alone in the hall. Joel found the mitten straightaway. He hid it in a more obscure place. She came back.

"Have you found it?"

"Not yet," said Joel. "But it must be here."

"Tell me when you've got it," she said, leaving him on his own again.

The wireless was on in the living room. Joel pretended to be searching, and peeped cautiously into the room. She was sitting on the sofa, painting her nails. Joel watched in fascination. He screwed up his eyes and made her look slightly blurred. He could almost believe that she was wearing transparent veils. With nothing on underneath.

He didn't know how long he stood watching her, but it suddenly dawned on him that she'd seen him. She stood up and Joel produced the mitten.

"What are you looking at?" she asked.

She didn't sound angry.

"I don't know," said Joel. "But I've found my mitten. It was lying underneath a scarf."

A look of surprise flitted across her face. But then she smiled.

"No doubt it was," she said.

"I'll be going now, then," said Joel.

He didn't want to leave. But he didn't have any more lost mittens to search for.

"How's Digby?"

"He's fine. His temperature's normal again now."

She had already opened the door. Joel was stamping his feet as if to keep warm.

"Is there anything else you want?"

"No," said Joel. "Nothing else."

Then he left. On the way home he thought about how well it had gone. Now he could go to the shop and show the fat old women that he knew the new assistant. And no doubt he'd be able to find another excuse to visit her again.

The guitar, he thought. I must start practicing tomorrow.

He was in a hurry. He hardly had time to pause outside the windows of the shoe shop and take another look at the boots he wanted Samuel to buy for him. They were expensive. But Joel knew that there were others that cost even more. Those were the ones he would try on first when they went to the shop together. Say how good they were. But Samuel would have none of that when he heard the price. At which point Joel would try on the ones he really wanted to have. And he would get them. Because they were cheaper.

By the time he reached home Samuel was already asleep. As he walked up the stairs Joel had felt worried again, in case Samuel had gone out drinking. But the snores he heard were like music in his ears.

He sat for a while on the edge of his bed, holding Simon's guitar in his hands. It was dirty. That was something he hadn't noticed before. But there again, everything in Simon's house was dirty. He fetched a rag from the kitchen and started polishing. Before long the guitar was gleaming bright. He leaned it against the wall where he could see it from his bed. Then he crept down under the covers.

The day had started badly. But it finished rather better. Tomorrow he would be at his desk when school started. In the afternoon he would go round to Kringström's and start playing.

He closed his eyes. Felt how tired he was.

And now he could locate Captain Joel Gustafson. It was easy now.

The storm has abated. The mutineers have been defeated. The lookout has reported that an unusual-looking bird has perched on the figurehead on the bow of the ship. That means they are approaching land.

Despite his painful injuries, Captain Gustafson has gone up on deck. One of his ankles has been injured in the battle with the mutineers. Now the warm wind is blowing into his face. Soon they will reach the shore . . . .

Joel fell asleep.

In his dreams he drifted out into his sea where the breakers were rolling slowly.

Back and forth. Back and forth . . .

— THIRTEEN —

The next day Joel turned up at school on time, at last.

It had snowed during the night. The school caretaker had started making a skating rink on the big expanse of gravel next to the playground. Winter had really set in now. Otto and Joel glared at each other during the breaks, but both the headmaster and Miss Nederström were keeping a close eye on them.

During one of the breaks the Greyhound came up to talk to Joel. That made him suspicious straightaway. She'd never done that before.

"No doubt you've told everybody that I'm going to learn to play the guitar," he said accusingly.

"I haven't said a word," she said. "I don't spread gossip."

Joel knew that wasn't true. Nobody ran around

spreading as much gossip as the Greyhound. Joel thought that might be because she could run so fast. She was a gossip runner.

But now he wasn't so sure. Maybe it was true after all? But if so, he didn't understand why.

As soon as school was over he hurried home to fetch the guitar. On the way he called in at Ehnström's shop to buy potatoes and butter. He ran his hand through his hair before going in, but he was out of luck. It was Ehnström himself behind the counter. He could see Sonja in the storeroom, and tried to draw out his purchases for as long as possible. But the old ladies were jostling him from behind. He would have to wait until the next day before greeting her.

When he got to the block of flats where Kringström lived he was soaked in sweat. He had to pause and recover his breath before going up the stairs. The black van used by the orchestra was parked outside. Today there was no risk of Kringström having gone to Brunflo.

Kringström opened the door with a clarinet in his hand. Music could be heard in the background.

"'Siam Blues,'" said Kringström. "Come on in."

Then he stood in the hall playing to the record while Joel was taking off his outdoor clothes. Halfway through he changed from the clarinet to a big bass saxophone. Joel listened in fascination. Kringström really could play.

Joel looked at the man's hands. His fingers were short

and stubby, but even so he could reach all the keys he needed to press.

The music came to an end. Kringström put down the saxophone. They had come into the biggest room, where all the music stands were. Joel sat on the floor and took the guitar out of its case. Kringström picked it up and examined it carefully. Joel worried in case it wasn't good enough.

"Where have you got this from?" Kringström asked.

"I've borrowed it," said Joel.

"It's a fine old guitar," said Kringström. "They don't make them like this anymore. If they did they'd be worth many thousands of kronor."

The very thought made Joel feel dizzy. Simon had had that guitar hanging on his wall for as long as Joel had known him. No doubt he had no idea that it was so valuable.

"But the strings are in poor condition," said Kringström. "We'd better start by changing them."

"I haven't got any others," said Joel.

Kringström shrugged.

"But I have. If you lead an orchestra you need to be equipped like a car repair shop. Spare parts for all the instruments."

He produced a new set of strings. Joel watched him removing the old ones and fixing the new ones. Then Kringström nodded towards the piano.

"Give me a C," he said.

Joel didn't know where to find a C. He was forced to ask.

"The white key that comes immediately before two black ones," said Kringström, sounding only a little bit annoyed.

Joel prodded at a C.

"You don't need to belt it as hard as that," said Kringström.

Joel tapped the key once more. More gently this time. And Kringström tuned the guitar.

Then he handed it to Joel, and they started to practice.

After an hour Joel had a pain in his fingers and his back and his wrists. He didn't see how he'd ever be able to learn. Even if he could it would take so long that he'd be in the churchyard before he could play a single Elvis song. Kringström pulled at Joel's fingers, told him to bend his wrist more and to press harder. The strings cut into the tips of Joel's fingers.

"You'll learn eventually," said Kringström when the hour was up. "But it will take time."

He told Joel what he ought to practice before the next time they met.

"I haven't time for more than two lessons a week," said Kringström. "And now we must decide how you're going to pay."

A shudder ran down Joel's spine.

Did Kringström want paying? He'd thought Kringström did this kind of thing because it was fun.

Kringström noticed Joel's panic. His face broke into a large smile. Joel had never seen anything like it before. Kringström looking happy.

"You can help me to clean," he said. "I don't want money. But you can dust down the records and music stands. And wash up when necessary. Do you know how to wash up?"

"Yes," said Joel. "And I can clean as well."

"Boys can't usually do that kind of thing," said Kringström.

"But I can," said Joel.

Kringström nodded.

"That's settled, then. You needn't bother today. We'll start next time. One hour with the guitar, then one hour with the dishcloth and duster."

Joel put his guitar back in its case and got ready to leave. By then Kringström had already put on a new record and started playing. This time he had taken up position behind a big double bass. Joel stood in the doorway, watching. Listening. Kringström played away and seemed to have forgotten already that Joel was there.

As Joel emerged through the front door, the Greyhound appeared from behind the corner. Joel had the impression that she'd been lying in wait for him. He was on his guard immediately. What did she want now?

"Can you play yet?" she asked.

"You know full well that it takes time," said Joel. "With your wrists and your fingers and all that. How many notes do you think have to be learnt?"

Joel set off walking. She accompanied him. There's something she wants, Joel thought. But I'm not going to ask her what.

They walked down the hill in silence. Now and then she would run for a few feet, circling round Joel. She really was like a dog. She couldn't keep still.

"Why didn't you tell the truth?" she asked without warning.

Joel stopped. What did she mean?

"Why didn't you say that you didn't go to school because your dad was drunk?"

Joel stared at her.

"He wasn't at all."

"What was he, then?"

"He was ill."

Joel could feel his cheeks burning. Nobody had permission to say that his dad was drunk. Even if it was true. And how did the Greyhound know about it anyway?

"If you'd told the truth you needn't have been in detention. And you didn't need to say it in front of the class. You could have waited until one of the breaks."

"My dad was ill," said Joel, and set off walking again. The Greyhound followed him remorselessly.

Joel stopped again.

"How do you know about it?" he asked. "Did you see him?"

"I just know," she said, continuing to circle round Joel.

There could only be one explanation, Joel thought. The

Greyhound gossips more than anybody else in town, but that must also mean that she knows more than anybody else. The gossip has to come from somewhere, even for her.

Joel started walking again. Faster now.

"He doesn't drink very often," Joel said. "Less and less, in fact."

They had come to the bottom of the hill. Joel thought the Greyhound would turn round now and run back home. But she didn't. She carried on walking by his side.

Joel was less suspicious now. The Greyhound hadn't spat out her comments as she usually did. It was almost as if he'd started to enjoy walking along in her company. Quite apart from the fact that she could run faster than anybody else, she was rather pretty. And not stupid. Joel could think of much worse company than her.

They had come as far as the Community Center. Joel hadn't the slightest idea where the thought came from— all too often he spoke first and thought later. This was one of those occasions.

The poster in the case outside the entrance, advertising the film being shown that week, didn't look especially exciting. A man and a woman in old-fashioned clothes stood with their arms around each other, staring in horror at something that couldn't possibly be guessed. Joel assumed it was a love story. But nevertheless, as it was for adults only, there might be something exciting in the film.

"Would you like to go to the pictures?" he asked, pointing at the poster.

"It's adults only," said the Greyhound.

"I know how to get in even so," said Joel. "Without paying as well."

"I don't believe that for a moment," she said.

But Joel could see that she was interested already.

"Do you want to go to the pictures or don't you?" he asked.

"I do."

"But you must promise not to tell anybody how I get in."

"I promise."

"If you tell anybody, everybody will start doing what I do. And Engman will find out. Then it won't be possible anymore."

Engman was the cinema caretaker. So far he hadn't found out that Joel knew a way of getting in without paying, no matter if the film was adults only or not. He'd discovered how to do it during the many evenings he'd been out in the streets looking for the dog that was heading for a distant star. Ture had been with him the first time. But since Ture moved away, Joel had always been on his own. And now here he was inviting the Greyhound to come with him. He didn't understand it himself.

The film began at half past seven. There was only one showing. Joel pointed to a car repair shop on the other side of the street.

"You must be there by a quarter past seven," he said. "And don't say a word to anybody."

She promised. Then she ran off home. Joel stood watching her, racing along the street like a flash of lightning.

For a brief moment Joel tried to imagine the Greyhound dressed in transparent veils. With nothing on underneath. But the thought horrified him.

Then he set off home. It was high time he started to make dinner.

Samuel came home. And he was sober. As they ate Joel kept glancing at him surreptitiously. Samuel seemed to be back to normal now. After dinner he sat in the armchair by the wireless, leafing through the newspaper. Joel went to his room and did what Kringström had told him to do. He would have to practice every day. Otherwise he'd never learn. As seven o'clock approached he got ready to go out. Samuel lowered his newspaper and looked at him.

"Are you going out again?"

"I'm just going to return some books to the library."

"But you were there only a couple of days ago."

"I read a lot."

"Show me what you're reading!"

Joel went back to his room and fetched a book. One that he hadn't finished reading yet. *Mutiny on the Bounty.* He knew what it was about, though. An old sailing ship whose crew set the captain adrift in a dinghy and left him to survive as best he could.

Samuel looked at the cover and read the blurb on the back.

"Maybe that's something for me as well. I ought to read more books than I do. All I do is sleep."

"You can borrow it," said Joel.

Then he went out. At exactly seven o'clock he was in place in the shadows on the other side of the Community Center. Engman was just opening the doors and switching on the lights in the foyer. His wife was in the ticket office. People hadn't started to arrive yet. Joel suspected that there wouldn't be many in the audience. The posters were not very alluring. And there were no well-known stars in the film. The projectionist appeared. His name was Tunström and he was really a butcher, but he'd been the projectionist all the time Joel knew anything about it. He sometimes fell asleep in his booth. When that happened, his snores used to echo round the auditorium.

Joel gave a start. The Greyhound had appeared by his side. She was red in the face. Joel guessed she must have run all the way from home. How long would that have taken her? One minute?

"We have to wait here," Joel said.

"Are you sure you're not making it up?"

"Go home if you don't believe me."

She stayed put. Asked no more questions.

It was approaching half past seven. Joel was right. Not many people had turned up. Engman was standing by the entrance doors, looking not best pleased.

"It's probably a bad film," Joel said. "Still, it's adults only."

Half past seven. One minute past. Engman stepped out into the street and looked up and down. Then he closed the door.

It was time.

"Just follow me," said Joel. "And be as quiet as you can."

Joel led her quickly over the street and into the courtyard at the back of the Community Center. He groped his way along the wall in the shadows. The Greyhound was just behind him. He came to the stairs leading down into the basement. Carefully, he took hold of the door. If he lifted it up at the same time as pulling it towards him, it would open. Joel produced the flashlight he'd remembered to put in his pocket. The Greyhound looked scared.

"There's no cinema down there," she said.

"Are you coming or aren't you? The film will probably have started by now."

They crept into the darkness. Joel pointed the flashlight down at the floor. They could hear the sound from the screen, coming from up above. The Greyhound stayed close behind Joel. They tiptoed quietly up the stairs leading to the stage behind the screen. The Greyhound hesitated, but Joel pulled her along with him. Now they could see the pictures from behind. Joel peered cautiously into the auditorium through a slit in the screen. The upstairs seats seemed to be completely empty. He pointed to a staircase. When they got to the top Joel opened the door slowly. There was nobody there.

Every single seat was empty.

Joel pointed. They sat down in the front row.

The film had just started.

"What if Engman comes?"

"Why should he do that when there's nobody sitting upstairs?"

They started watching the film. It really was very boring. But the Greyhound giggled every time the actors kissed.

Joel leaned against the rail and looked down into the stalls. He'd heard noises coming from the entrance door: evidently some more people had turned up to watch this boring film.

He could see them now.

He gave a start. At first he thought he was seeing things. But no, he recognized who it was.

Sonja Mattsson. The shop assistant at Ehnström's.

And she was not alone. She had a man with her.

A man who sat down beside her, holding her hand.

Joel felt a pang of jealousy. More than jealousy. A feeling he didn't really recognize.

He leaned back. The Greyhound was watching the film.

But Joel couldn't concentrate.

All he could think about was the girl sitting downstairs.

— FOURTEEN —

The Greyhound giggled.

Now they were kissing again on the screen. Men and women, kissing each other. Some were kissing furtively, others openly, behind doors and sitting on horses. Long kisses and short kisses.

The Greyhound continued giggling.

Joel sat thinking about Sonja Mattsson in the seats down below. And about the unknown man who was holding her hand.

It was as if the film was really about Joel. Even if he wasn't kissing anybody. A woman engaged to a captain in the U.S. cavalry was meeting another man in secret. That was what the film was about. Joel had gathered that much. He realized that he was overwhelmed with jealousy. He was the one who ought to have been sitting downstairs beside

Sonja Mattsson. Not somebody else, some totally unknown person.

But there again, he had nothing against sitting here upstairs next to the Greyhound. When he thought about the possibility of changing places with the unknown man down below, that wasn't a good idea either.

Joel leaned forward over the rail. Sonja was still holding the unknown man's hand.

"What are you looking at?" whispered the Greyhound.

"I don't want to end up walking with a stoop," Joel hissed back. "I have to keep stretching."

He tried to concentrate on what was happening on the screen. There was still lots of kissing going on. He wondered if he ought to take hold of the Greyhound's hand. But he was unsure of how she would react. Would she start screaming? Would she hit him? He decided it was best not to try it.

The film was boring. There were groans and moans and creaking noises down below in the stalls. The only one sitting absolutely still and staring at all the people kissing everybody else was the Greyhound. Joel thought it might be an idea to take the opportunity of kissing the Greyhound. He didn't know how to do it, but perhaps she wouldn't notice that. She'd just think it was a part of the film. If he did it really quickly.

Without another thought he leaned towards her, took hold of her shoulders and pressed his lips against her.

He could feel her lips against his. They tasted sweet.

Then he drew back. But she didn't scream. She didn't giggle either. Joel thought she didn't even look annoyed. Even if it was hard to see her face properly in the darkness.

"What are you doing, are you out of your mind? Stop it," said the Greyhound.

"Come on, it was no big deal," said Joel, who still hadn't understood what he'd done.

"You can't," said the Greyhound.

"Can't what?"

"Kiss. Watch the film and learn."

"You can teach me, if you're so good at it."

"Yes, I can. But not now."

Joel tried to concentrate on the film again. Had the Greyhound really meant what she said? That she could teach him how to kiss? Perhaps the Greyhound knew about all the things that Otto used to talk about? Knew properly?

He looked sideways at her. She was watching what was going on in the film, but she noticed immediately that he was looking at her.

"Stop it," she said angrily.

Joel looked away immediately. Now she sounded annoyed. He would have to be careful to avoid making her change her mind.

Joel started thinking about Sonja Mattsson again. Who was this man she had come to the cinema with? Was he also somebody who had moved here from Stockholm?

He'd better not come up here and take hold of the Greyhound's hand.

Thoughts were racing around inside his head. All at once there was so much to keep a check on.

On the screen they were still riding horses, burning down beautiful big white houses and kissing behind doors. Joel was now really interested. He tried hard to see how they did it.

He'd realized that one thing was very important: you had to close your eyes while kissing.

Maybe that was something he could teach the Greyhound. So that he didn't give the impression of being completely ignorant.

Joel suddenly had the impression that the film was approaching its end. This was always a snag with going to the cinema without paying: you never got to see the end. You had to be outside when Engman switched the lights on. Otherwise there could be trouble.

"We'll have to go now," he said to the Greyhound.

"Can't we see the end?"

"I'm afraid not. Engman puts the lights on as soon as the film's over and so we have to be gone by then."

He could see even in the darkness that she was far from pleased. He started to worry that she no longer wanted to teach him how to kiss.

Joel stood up.

"It'll be finished in a minute," he said. "I think we have to go."

"What's the point of going to the pictures if you can't see how the film ends?" she said.

"All the endings are the same," said Joel. "You can work it out for yourself."

They went back the same way as they'd come in. Just as they were passing the back of the screen the film ended. But they managed to get out through the basement door before Engman switched the lights on.

They stood outside in the dark. Joel waited until all the people who had seen the film had gone their various ways. But he didn't see Sonja Mattsson and the unknown man. They must have gone off in the opposite direction, out of sight from where he was standing. He waited until Engman had closed the doors with a bang before starting to move away himself. They left the back courtyard and emerged into the street.

"It wasn't much of a film," said Joel.

Needless to say, the Greyhound thought it was good. He ought to have expected that.

"It was pretty good, surely you could see that?"

Joel held his ground, even though he had begun to wonder.

"There wasn't enough action," he said. "They just stood around, talking."

"What's wrong with that? Besides, they were speaking English."

Joel couldn't think of any more reasons why he thought the film was no good.

155

"I've seen better films," he said lamely.

They started walking. But not in the direction of Joel's house, nor hers. Without Joel understanding why, he suddenly wondered if Lars Olson, lying dead in the churchyard, would have thought the film was any good or not.

They stopped in front of the shoe shop windows.

"I'm going to get a new pair of boots," said Joel.

"Provided your dad doesn't drink up the money first," said the Greyhound.

Joel stared at her. He thought he ought to hit her. Or rub snow all over her.

Then he saw that she regretted having said that. She put her hand over her mouth.

"I didn't mean it."

"Why did you say it, then?"

"I don't know."

They continued walking. Joel felt more sad than angry. If he was angry, it was with Samuel. Who didn't know how to behave.

"I have to say the film was really pretty bad," said the Greyhound.

"I've seen worse," said Joel.

Joel kept on walking by her side, and waiting. He hadn't forgotten what she said about Samuel, but he was waiting for her to start teaching him. They walked past the bank and the pharmacy and the Highways Department yard with all the excavators and road graders. Eventually Joel couldn't hold back any longer.

"Aren't you going to teach me, then?" he asked.

The Greyhound giggled.

"Here? Out in the street?"

"Why not?"

"It's too cold."

"I've seen films in which people stand at the North Pole and kiss each other."

"Why don't you go there, then?"

"Where shall we go?"

She didn't reply. Joel could see that she was trying to make up her mind. He realized that it was best to say nothing, and wait.

"There'll be nobody in at my place tomorrow night," she said. "So you can come round. But if you mention it to anybody, I'll tell everybody that your dad's a drunkard."

Joel was about to reply, but then he realized that she'd vanished. In a flash. There was no point in trying to catch up with her.

He started walking home. He was already looking forward to tomorrow night. That feeling was there again, he wasn't at all sure what it was. It would be hard to wait. He sometimes wished days could simply be whisked away. That two evenings could follow one after the other, with nothing in between.

He stopped dead.

I'm me and nobody else, he thought. What happens to me happens only to me.

It was only a few nights since the first snow had crept up on him without a sound. Then he'd made his New Year resolutions. He'd already tried sleeping out in the snow. And he'd borrowed a guitar worth a lot of money from Simon Windstorm. Kringström had started giving him lessons. Sonja Mattsson had allowed him into her flat. And now the Greyhound was going to teach him how to kiss.

Life was strange. For long periods nothing at all happened. And then everything happened all at once. Like an avalanche.

He started bouncing again. Bouncing along the street like a ball. He would eventually find out who had been holding Sonja Mattsson's hand. But first, the Greyhound would teach him how to kiss. And then he would no doubt persuade Sonja Mattsson to put on some transparent veils with nothing at all underneath.

He came to the house where he lived, and continued bouncing up the stairs.

And then he was overwhelmed by another avalanche.

An avalanche that was black and cold and made his stomach ache.

Samuel wasn't at home. He'd vanished again.

That could only mean one thing. He hadn't been able to resist. He'd gone out drinking again.

Joel smashed his fists down onto the kitchen table. He was so furious that he burst into tears. He didn't want Samuel for his father anymore. He wanted to be rid of him. He would put an ad in the local paper.

Inadequate father available for collection. N.B.—Free!

Or perhaps there were special rubbish dumps where you could dispose of inadequate parents? Where they could mix with others just as useless as they were?

Joel slumped down on the kitchen floor. Samuel had gone out again. And even if Joel had decided to wash his hands of him, he knew that before long he'd be obliged to go out looking for his dad.

He spoils everything for me, Joel thought. If I'm only a little bit cheerful, then of course he feels the need to go out and drink himself silly. I ought to go to bed out there in the snow and toughen myself up. Or practice the guitar. Instead, I have to go out looking for Samuel. It's not fair.

Joel stayed sitting there on the floor for ages. He wasn't furious anymore, just sad and tired. His stomach hurt. Samuel was there inside him, biting and chewing away. He stood up, went to Samuel's room and sat down on his chair. The newspaper was lying on the floor, his pipe on top of the wireless. Joel hadn't taken his boots off. Big pools of dirty water formed on the floor. But he didn't bother about that.

Mutiny on the Bounty was lying open next to the wireless. Joel leaned forward and reached for it. He noticed that somebody had underlined a few lines in pencil. It could only have been Samuel. Didn't he realize that you could be barred from borrowing library books if you drew or wrote in them? Who would it be who was banned? Him, of course. Joel. Not Samuel. Samuel would get away with it. Because he didn't know what he was doing when he was out drinking.

Joel read what his dad had underlined. Quickly at first, but then more slowly.

"Pitcairn Island, the island to which the mutineers, led by Fletcher, managed to get to, exists in reality. Even today descendants of the mutineers still live on the island."

Joel put the book down. Why had Samuel chosen to underline those very words? Joel had never heard anything about Samuel having visited that island when he was a sailor.

Joel went to fetch Samuel's big atlas of the world and all the deep oceans. Then he started looking. It took him ages. But in the end he found Pitcairn Island. A little dot in the middle of a boundless ocean. A totally isolated little dot far away from everything.

That's where Samuel ought to have gone, Joel thought. He might not have mutinied on a ship, but he has mutinied against me. He's left me all alone in a dinghy. He's gone away to Pitcairn Island. . . .

Joel suddenly started thinking. Was it possible that he was right? That Samuel had indeed had that idea? Of running away to Pitcairn Island? Just like Mummy Jenny had done all those years ago. Packed her bag and run away.

Joel knew there was only one thing to do. Look for him and ask.

Joel went out into the street. It was already late. No people about, no mutineers. Just empty, deserted streets. Joel tried to work out where Samuel might be. When it was as late as this, he would have to go to somebody's house in order to drink. To other drinkers. There were various possibilities. Down by the railway bridge there was a ramshackle old house where some of the boozers used to gather. Joel had fetched Samuel home from there several times in the past. Then there was another place next to the old dairy. He might well have gone there.

The house by the railway bridge was closest. Joel decided to start by looking there. Samuel was inside Joel's stomach, gnawing away. It hurt. There was nothing Joel found worse than having to fetch Samuel when he was surrounded by other drunks, all of them on the hard stuff.

When he got to the house there was an old man standing outside, peeing into the snow. Joel recognized him. His name was Anders Wedberg; he worked in a car repair shop and was liable to start fighting when he'd been drinking. Joel waited until he'd gone back in. Then he sneaked up to a window and peered inside. There were four men in there, round a table with bottles on it. But no Samuel. Joel moved on.

His boots were hurting something awful. Needless to say, Samuel wouldn't have any money left to buy Joel a pair of new ones. And to make things worse, Joel would get blood poisoning in his ankles if he had to be out every night, looking for Samuel.

He came to the house by the old dairy.

There was a wireless on inside. Or perhaps it was somebody singing? Joel crept up to a window and peeped in. A curtain was drawn and there was only a narrow crack to look through.

But that was more than enough.

Samuel was sitting there with a glass in his hand.

His body was swaying from side to side like a ship in a storm.

— FIFTEEN —

The hardest part was the last bit.

Taking tight hold of the handle until your knuckles turned white, opening the door and entering the oozing cloud of smoke. Joel could think of nothing worse. And now he was here again. To drag Samuel home.

His hope was that Samuel hadn't yet had time to become completely drunk. If he was, he could be difficult. Might ask Joel to wait outside while he took a few more swigs from the bottle. Try to delay things for as long as possible.

Joel counted to three, then opened the door. Four pairs of bloodshot eyes turned to look at him in apathetic surprise. Joel knew them all. Samuel had been to their place many times before. One of them was called the Crow, because of his big, pointed nose. The two other men in

163

the room were brothers, known as the Goblins. They looked like a pair of shaggy dogs. Both of them used to be lumberjacks. Nowadays they got by doing odd jobs for a day or two when they needed money.

"Have you come?" asked Samuel in surprise.

Joel noticed to his relief that Samuel wasn't yet so drunk that he wouldn't be able to stand up.

"Let's go home now," Joel said. "It's getting late."

Samuel nodded. Joel often had the impression that in fact, Samuel was glad his son had come to fetch him. He never drank to make himself happy. Possibly in order to be less sad.

"Stay for a bit longer," said the Crow, trying to take hold of Joel's arm. But Joel pushed him away. He'd been through that before.

Samuel rose unsteadily to his feet. Then he pulled himself together.

Joel had already turned and left the room. He didn't want to stay in that smoky atmosphere a second longer than necessary.

On the way home Samuel didn't say a single word. Neither did Joel. Samuel occasionally stumbled, but Joel never needed to grab hold of him to prevent him from falling down.

Joel tried to imagine that the man walking by his side was the captain of the *Bounty*. But no matter how hard he tried, it was Samuel. And his back seemed more hunched than ever.

When they got home Samuel slumped down onto one of the kitchen chairs.

"I couldn't help it," he said. "That business with Sara was not good."

Joel didn't bother to respond. He had enough trouble trying to take Samuel's boots off.

"It won't happen again," Samuel said.

Joel still didn't say anything, but by now he'd managed to get his father's boots off.

Samuel started to make coffee. That was a good sign, Joel knew that. It meant his dad wanted to be sober. Meanwhile Joel went to fetch the book in which Samuel had done the underlining. He sat down at the table and watched Samuel standing by the stove, waiting for the coffee to be ready.

Samuel sat down opposite him. He stank of spirits. Joel thought he looked like an animal that had forgotten to shave. If there had been any animals that shaved, of course.

Samuel drank his coffee. Joel knew his father had a guilty conscience, but he had no hesitation in exploiting it. Samuel deserved to pay for causing so much trouble all the time.

"Have you any money left for my boots?" he asked.

Samuel nodded.

"It's in the bureau."

Samuel sometimes told lies when he had a really guilty conscience, but on this occasion Joel believed him. That made everything so much easier. At least he hadn't managed to drink up Joel's boots.

Joel had survived the black avalanche yet again.

"Why have you made underlinings in this book?" he asked. "Don't you know that it's forbidden to write anything in books borrowed from the library?"

"I only wrote in pencil," said Samuel defensively. "It can be erased. But there was something I wanted to show you."

"I've already read it," said Joel. "About Pitcairn Island. And the mutineers who still live there."

"We ought to go there one of these days," said Samuel, and his bloodshot eyes took on a dreamy look. "Just you and me."

"Shall we row there?" wondered Joel. "Or shall we float there on a few logs?"

Samuel didn't seem to hear.

"We ought to go there," he said again. "Perhaps we could live there for a few years?"

"Is there a school there?"

Samuel still didn't hear him. He was sinking deeper and deeper into his dreams.

"Maybe it's time to move away from here," he said slowly. "Get away from all this snow and seek out some warm sand instead."

Joel wanted to believe that Samuel really meant what he said. But he didn't dare. He didn't want to be disappointed again. Like so many times before.

Samuel would stay in this house by the river and continue cutting down trees in the forest. Perhaps he would one day succeed in cutting down a path all the way to the sea. But Joel couldn't afford to wait all that time. If he really was going to get to Pitcairn Island, he would have to arrange it himself. Samuel would have to carry on traveling in his dreams. No doubt they would never make the journey together. Joel couldn't enter into Samuel's dream. And Samuel wouldn't be able to travel in reality.

That was the way it was. Joel could see it all clearly before him now.

He couldn't afford to be childish any longer.

First the Greyhound would teach him how to kiss. Then he would become a rock idol and get away from the winter and this dump of a little town and all the snow that fell silently during the night. He would leave enough money for Samuel, but he would have to arrange the journey to Pitcairn Island on his own. Possibly with somebody else.

Sonja Mattsson, perhaps.

Or the Greyhound?

Or maybe somebody else, but he didn't yet know who.

"I'm going to bed now," Joel said.

Samuel nodded.

"We both need to get some sleep," he said. "I'll stay at home tomorrow night. I promise."

Hmm, we'll see, Joel thought. But I'll have gone round

to the Greyhound's then. So I won't be going out looking for you.

But he knew that he would do so, if it was necessary.
That was the way it was.

The next day Joel was on time for school again. When
he woke up he'd felt so tired that he'd almost been
sick. But then he started to think about the coming
evening and the Greyhound and what was going to
happen. That livened him up and he jumped out of
bed. Samuel was getting shaved in the kitchen. His
eyes were less red now.

"Last night was the last time," he said. "Thank you for
coming to fetch me."

"When are we going to buy the new boots?" Joel
asked.

"It's Saturday tomorrow," said Samuel. "I'll leave work
early so that we have time to go to the shops."

He picked up his rucksack and left. Joel ate his sandwiches, and thought about how Sara ought to be made to
realize what she had set in motion. She ought to give
Samuel money, if his state made it necessary for him to
drink. She was the one responsible for what had happened.

In his thoughts Joel sent her to the rubbish dump for
inadequate grown-ups. Then he looked at the wall clock
and saw that he needed to set off for school.

The Greyhound was sitting in the desk next to Joel's,

giggling. That immediately made Joel wonder if she'd really meant what she'd promised the previous evening. But he didn't want to ask. That would only give him away.

Joel remained unsure until the last lesson. It was local history. Miss Nederström talked about what life by the river had been like in the old days. In Lars Olson's day, Joel thought.

The Greyhound suddenly slipped Joel a note on a folded scrap of paper. He opened it carefully and read:

Not before seven o'clock. They'll have gone by then.

So it was true! He looked at her. She giggled again. Joel put the note deep down in his pocket.

"Are you paying attention, Joel?" Miss Nederström asked suddenly.

She had sharp eyes. Not least when it came to keeping watch on Joel Gustafson.

"Yes," said Joel. "We're talking about what this town looked like in the days of Lars Olson."

"Who's Lars Olson?"

"His body is lying in the churchyard. But he used to live here."

The class started giggling. But for once, Miss Nederström was on Joel's side.

"I'm glad to see that you are following," she said briskly. "The rest of you ought to do the same."

After school the Greyhound vanished in a flash. Joel was also in a hurry. He would have to spend the whole afternoon scurrying around, doing things. First he would have to collect the guitar and then go to Kringström's place for his lesson. Then he'd have to take the guitar home before going back to the flat where the Greyhound was going to be in by herself. He would have to go to the same building twice. First the second floor, and then the third.

But he managed it all. Kringström was in a good mood and taught Joel three chords. For the first time Joel had the feeling that, despite everything, he might be able to learn to play the guitar after all. Even if it still sounded pretty awful, even if his fingers were too short and his wrist wasn't as supple as it ought to be.

After the lesson Joel spent exactly an hour dusting down gramophone records and washing up. Then he rushed home with the guitar and made dinner. Samuel came home as usual and his eyes were not bloodshot anymore.

"I'm going to read your book tonight," he said. "Or shall we read it aloud?"

"I can't," said Joel. "I'm going out."

"Out again already?"

"I was more or less at home last night," Joel said, "but then I had to go out looking for you. That doesn't count."

That hit home. Samuel said nothing more.

Joel went to his room and lay down on the bed. He felt nervous. Perhaps the Greyhound would greet him wearing transparent veils. What would he do then?

He sat up with a start. He must get washed. Preferably have a bath. And change his clothes. And wet his comb and run it through his hair. And brush his teeth. That was the most important thing.

He would have to give the bath a miss. Samuel would wonder what on earth was going on if he took out the bathtub and put it in the middle of the kitchen floor on a weekday. Having a good wash would have to do. He rushed to the toilet and got undressed. Washed and scrubbed the whole of his body. Brushed his teeth until his gums started bleeding. Then he put on clean under-wear and his best pants. His ankles hurt where he had sores, but he would be getting new boots tomorrow. By then he'd have also learnt how to kiss. His body almost boiled over at the very thought.

Half past six. He called in on Samuel, who was sitting in his chair with the book in his hands. But he'd fallen asleep. And he was still only on page one.

Joel waited in the darkness outside the Greyhound's block of flats until he was sure it was at least a quarter past seven. Then he went up the stairs, past Kringström's flat, where he could hear the sound of a cheerful trombone, and stopped outside the Greyhound's door. *Alexandersson*, it said on the name-plate. Joel ran his hand through his hair once again, then rang the bell. Then he wanted to run away. But it was too late. The Greyhound opened the door. Joel noticed straightaway that she had painted her lips. They were very red.

"Are you just going to stand there?" she asked. "Or are you coming in?"

"Have your parents left?" Joel asked.

"They're playing bridge," she said.

Joel went in. He hoped she wouldn't ask him what bridge was. He wouldn't be able to tell her.

"Take your shoes off," she said. "We can't have you making the floor dirty."

Joel did as asked, then followed her into the living room. It was a big flat, full of beautiful furniture. Joel knew that the Greyhound's dad was a public prosecutor. He wasn't at all sure what that meant. But he did know that a public prosecutor earned a lot more money than a lumberjack like Samuel.

"You can't stay long," she said. "I'll teach you how to kiss, but then you'll have to go."

Joel could feel himself blushing. He had no idea what to do.

The Greyhound put a chair in the middle of the floor. Joel noticed that she was nervous as well. All the time she kept glancing towards the hall, as if she were afraid that her parents might come back again.

"Sit down on the chair," she said. "And purse your lips."

Joel did as he was told. She pouted as well, to show him how it was done. Joel tried to copy her. It felt stupid.

"Purse your lips more," she said. "And open your mouth. I assume you know how to give a peck?"

Joel pouted for all he was worth.

"You have to close your eyes as well," said the Greyhound, and demonstrated. She pursed her lips, put her head on one side and closed her eyes. Joel did the same.

Joel didn't like sitting on a chair in the middle of the floor. Something felt wrong, although he couldn't put his finger on it.

"Shouldn't we start now?" he asked.

"Start what?"

"Kissing."

"It's like with the guitar. You have to practice first."

Joel thought she was right.

"Close your eyes and purse your lips," she said. "And no peeping. Don't stop until I tell you to."

Joel did as she said. He thought it was lasting for a very long time. The Greyhound was giggling. But still she didn't say anything. Joel tried to imagine what it would be like, feeling her lips against his.

"Now you can open them," said the Greyhound.

Joel opened his eyes.

There were three of the Greyhound's friends standing in front of him. Plus two other boys from his class. When Joel opened his eyes they burst out laughing. Joel was petrified. He didn't understand what was happening at first. He was confused and started laughing as well.

Then it dawned on him that the Greyhound had made a fool of him.

He felt the tears welling up in his eyes.

He jumped up from his chair and launched himself in the direction of the hall. He grabbed hold of his outdoor clothes and his boots and raced out through the door in his socks. He could hear them all roaring with laughter. He didn't even stop to put his boots on. All that mattered was to get as far away as possible as quickly as possible.

A window opened somewhere in the building behind him. The laughter caught up with him. He ran down the hill in his stocking feet and didn't stop until he couldn't hear the laughter anymore. Only then did he put his boots on.

He stood there motionless.

Everything was still confused. He didn't know what had happened. But deep down inside everything was clear. The Greyhound had made a fool of him. She had planned it all. Her friends had been waiting in another room. That was why she had kept on glancing towards the hall all the time.

Joel could picture it all in front of him. How he was sitting there with his head on one side, pouting.

He was so embarrassed. What had happened was so awful that he couldn't even feel angry.

He trudged slowly home.

But he thought he might just as well lie down in the snow and die.

— SIXTEEN —

When Joel got home he went to the woodshed and sat down on the bed that was inside there. The cold steel springs hurt, but he sat there even so. He even lay down, and thought that he might as well carry on lying there until he had frozen to death.

Eventually he went into the house and up the stairs. He didn't really care if Samuel was at home or if he'd gone wandering off again. But in fact Samuel was in bed, asleep. The bedside light was still on. *Mutiny on the Bounty* was lying at the side of the bed. Joel switched the light off. Then he went to his own room and undressed. He crept between the sheets and pulled the covers over his head. Forced himself to stop thinking about what had happened.

Next to his ear he could hear a mouse gnawing away

inside the wall. If he'd been able to, Joel would have liked to crawl into the wall and take up residence there. He would never come out again. He would live inside that wall until he was a hundred years old and didn't need to live any longer.

He curled up. Kept thoughts from entering his head. And went to sleep.

Joel woke up with a start. He remembered immediately what had happened the previous night at the Greyhound's place. He tried to tell himself that it had only been a dream. That it hadn't really happened. But he couldn't get away from facts. He had sat on that chair and the Greyhound's friends had sneaked into the room.

Joel checked his alarm clock. He would soon have to get up and go to school. The Greyhound and her friends would all be there. And they would tell the rest of the class all about it. Tell the whole school. Joel had made a fool of himself.

He felt a stabbing pain in his stomach. He couldn't go to school. He would never be able to go back there for the rest of his life. As Samuel was like he was, Joel would be forced to leave town on his own. It was Saturday today. Tomorrow the night train would stop at the station, the one in which he used to post his secret letters. Tomorrow he would sneak aboard himself. He would hide away and listen as the train clattered over the railway bridge, and by the time it was morning again he would be many miles away. Then he would change his name, dye his hair a different color and become somebody else. Joel Gustafson wouldn't exist anymore. The Greyhound and her friends would laugh in vain.

Samuel suddenly appeared in the doorway.

"You'd better get up now or you'll be late for school," he said.

"I'm coming," said Joel.

"There's a storm brewing," said Samuel. "A snowstorm."

Joel hoped the whole town would be blown away.

"We'll buy your new boots today," said Samuel with a smile. "Assuming we're not snowed in."

"Yes," muttered Joel.

"Let's meet at twelve o'clock outside the shoe shop," said Samuel. "I'll be there on time. And have the money with me. Make sure you don't blow away."

He went back to the kitchen. Joel stayed in bed with the quilt up to his chin. He didn't want any new boots anymore. It didn't matter. He might as well carry on wearing the ones he had. In the end the sores would result in his feet dropping off. Or he would get blood poisoning and die in full view of whoever was interested. The Greyhound. And Miss Nederström. And all the rest of them.

But he couldn't just stay in bed. Samuel would start wondering. He got up and dressed. Samuel was about to put on his fur cap.

"Twelve noon," he said again. "Outside the shoe shop."

Joel listened to him walking downstairs. Once, Samuel had walked around on the decks of various ships. Now he just walked up and down stairs. Year after year. While his back became more and more hunched.

Joel went to sit on the window seat. It had become colder. Minus six degrees. And Samuel was right. It was windy. The overhead streetlight was swaying back and forth. There was a whistling noise in the walls. Cold air was forcing its way in through badly fitting windows. He shuddered when he pressed his cheek against the window-pane.

In the street down below people were struggling into the headwind that was raging in a series of powerful gusts. Young and old, everybody struggled. They were lit up intermittently by the streetlights. It was still dark. Everybody was on the way somewhere. Except Joel. He was sitting on the window seat, wondering if he ought to move into the wall and share living space with the mouse gnawing away inside there. He checked the time. The first lesson had already begun. Miss Nederström had noticed that Joel Gustafson was absent again. And the Greyhound was sitting with her friends, giggling. Perhaps they had already started passing round notes, telling everybody what had happened the previous evening.

Joel pressed his hands against his stomach. It hurt. Now it wasn't Samuel sitting inside there, gnawing away. It was the Greyhound.

Joel went back to bed. He lay under the covers fully dressed. He didn't know what to do. He'd been shown up. The only possibility was to go away. To disappear without a trace. They would write about him in the newspapers.

Joel Gustafson, who disappeared in mysterious circumstances . . .

The Joel Gustafson case . . .

The boy who went up in smoke . . .

He would sit on Pitcairn Island, reading what it said in the newspapers. But by then he wouldn't be called Joel anymore. His name was Fletcher. And he would have married the descendant of one of the old mutineers. She had come walking towards him along the beach one morning, wearing transparent veils. She resembled the Greyhound. But her lips were redder. And she ran even faster than the Greyhound. They already had a son called Joel. Joel Fletcher. Nobody would know that it was him, Joel Gustafson, who had once sat on a chair, pursing his lips.

His stomach ached less when he was dreaming. But it was hard to keep the dream going. It was trying to run away from him all the time. And then the Greyhound was back again, with all her laughing friends.

Joel knew he couldn't stay at home. But where could he go?

He stood by the window. It was blowing a gale now. And it had started snowing.

Simon, he thought. The only person I can go to is Simon Windstorm. I can't go to Gertrud's. She would see straight through me and start asking questions. And I don't want to answer them.

He put on his outdoor clothes. It was good that a storm was raging. Nobody would notice him out in the streets. Not even the headmaster, who had very sharp eyes. Everybody would be ducking into the wind and staring straight down the hill.

He went out into the wind. It really was blowing hard. He had to fight hard against it. But he'd made up his mind: he was going to go to Simon's house. He could be in peace there. He'd be able to plan his escape to Pitcairn Island. The journey that would begin the next day when he sneaked aboard the night train. Samuel could stand waiting for him outside the shoe shop in vain. He needed the money earmarked for the boots for his journey. He would borrow it from Samuel. In secret, while he was asleep. As it would be Sunday, he wouldn't be able to suggest that they go out to buy the boots. And he wouldn't notice that the money was missing. Eventually Joel would pay back the money many times over. For every krona he had borrowed, he would pay back a thousand.

He was passing the railway station now. The bus to Ljusdal was about to leave. The windshield wipers were straining to keep the snow off so that the driver could see. Joel thought about the time he'd fallen under that very bus, and avoided being killed thanks to a miracle. Now he wondered if it might have been as well if the bus had killed him. At least he wouldn't have had to sit on that confounded chair that the Greyhound had put out for him.

The wind howled, the snow whirled. Joel kept on struggling. He was past the hospital now. On his way out of town. There were already high drifts on the road. Before long it would be impassable. Cars would get stuck in the drifts and would have to stay there until the snow-plow got through to them.

Joel very nearly missed the turnoff to Simon's house. He had to wade through the snow. The old truck was parked outside, half covered by snow. He came to the house and banged on the door. No reply. He opened it and went in.

The house was empty. Simon wasn't at home. Nor were the dogs. There was a faint glow in the wood-burning stove. Joel brushed off the snow and stood by the stove to warm his hands. Where could Simon and the dogs have gone to? The truck was parked outside. And Simon wasn't the type to go for a walk if it wasn't necessary. If he needed to go somewhere he would take the truck.

Joel had the distinct impression that there was something wrong. He put his wooly hat and his mittens back on and went outside again. There was no sign of any footsteps, neither from Simon nor the dogs. They had been snowed over. Joel waded over to the truck and managed to open one of the doors that had almost frozen fast. There was nothing inside apart from Simon's cockerel, staring at him. Joel closed the door again and peered round. The storm was getting worse. The snow made it almost impossible for him to see. He shouted for Simon. No answer. There was a roaring sound from the fir trees, which were bent almost double in the wind. He shouted again. Still no answer.

Then he gave a start. Something had touched him. He wheeled round. It was one of Simon's dogs. It was whining. Joel bent down and patted it on the head. Then he looked round. Where was the other dog? And where was Simon?

"Where's Simon?" he asked the dog. "Simon? Where's Simon?"

The dog whined. Joel was worried. Now he was sure that something had happened.

Joel took a few steps to one side and beckoned to the dog. It remained where it was, whining. Joel moved a bit farther away. At which point the dog started running off. Joel followed it. It vanished into the forest. Joel had trouble keeping up. He stumbled and staggered forward as best he could. He was already sweaty and out of breath. The wind was different in there among the trees. And not so much snow was falling through all the branches. But the roaring sound from the fir trees was just as loud. It sounded like a raging fire. A snow fire and a storm fire. The dog kept on leading the way, with Joel close behind. He wondered if he'd be able to retrace his steps. But the dog was there in front of him. The dog knew where it was going.

All of a sudden, it stopped. Joel caught up with it. There was the other dog. And Simon. Stretched out in the snow. An axe was lying next to one of his hands. Joel knelt down and shook him. But Simon didn't open his eyes. Joel wondered in horror if he was dead. He shook Simon harder and shouted his name. The dogs howled. Simon groaned faintly. Joel couldn't see any sign of an injury. But on the other hand, it looked as if Simon had been sick. Joel had no idea what to do. If only Samuel had been there. This was too much for Joel to manage on his own. Simon was ill. He might even be dying. Joel tried to think. Should he run for help? But the dogs would stay with Simon. Joel might not be able to find his way out of the forest. The footprints in the snow were already disappearing. There was only one possibility. He would have to carry or drag Simon back to the house. Then Joel would be able to make a fire in the stove. Simon could lie in bed and keep warm while Joel ran for help. He bent down and tried to lift Simon up. But he was too heavy. So Joel took hold of his arms and started dragging him. He pulled as hard as he could, and managed to move Simon a few feet.

This is impossible, he thought in desperation.

But it had to be possible. And Joel kept on pulling.

He didn't know how long it took him to get to Simon's house, but it must have been several hours. Joel had fallen over lots of times, from sheer exhaustion. But every time, he'd scrambled up again and carried on pulling. When they got to the cottage he was so exhausted that he was sick. But he managed to summon up his last reserves of strength to drag Simon indoors and into his bed. Then he lit the stove. His fingers were as stiff as knitting needles. There was no feeling in them. But he didn't wait to get warm. As soon as the fire in the stove had taken, he started running to the road, which was completely blocked now. The storm continued thundering all around him. The fir trees were doubling over as if somebody were standing behind them, whipping them. Joel forced his way forward through the snow, little by little, and hoped that a car would come past. It was pitch-black now, and he was so tired that he wouldn't be able to keep going for much longer. He sat down to rest in a snowdrift. But just as he was about to fall asleep, he woke up with a start. If he dozed off in the snow, he would die. He forced himself to stand up and kept on walking.

Eventually he heard it. The sound of something different in the storm. Then he saw a flashing light between the trees. He stood in the middle of the road and waved his arms about. It was a truck with a snowplow attachment heading towards him. And it stopped. Somebody climbed out of the cab and came towards him.

"It's Simon," said Joel. "He's ill. He needs help."

He had only a vague memory of what happened next. But somebody helped him up into the cab, where it was warm. A voice he didn't recognize asked for his name and address.

"You must fetch Simon," Joel said. "I found him in the forest. He's ill. I think he's dying."

Joel thought he could hear another snowplow stopping right behind them. He heard several voices and saw flashlights shining. They disappeared into the forest, towards where Simon lived.

They've got to fetch him, Joel thought.

Then he remembered nothing else until the truck came to a halt outside his own house.

Joel looked at the driver. He knew who it was. His name was Nilsson, and he was reserve goalkeeper on the local ice hockey team. Whenever he played, the team nearly always lost.

"Is there anybody in?" Nilsson asked.

"Samuel," replied Joel.

"Can you manage on your own now?"

"How's Simon?"

"He's in the hospital. Can you manage on your own?"

"Yes," said Joel. "I always manage on my own."

He clambered out of the cab. His legs were so stiff that he could hardly bend his knees. He shuffled slowly up the stairs. When he entered the kitchen he could hear that

Samuel was asleep. The wall clock told him that it was eleven o'clock already.

There was a note on the kitchen table.

I'm not standing for any more of this running around late at night. Samuel. Weren't we supposed to buy some new boots today?

Joel sat down on the kitchen floor and took off all his clothes. He had big wounds on his hands. He didn't have the strength to get washed. All he could manage was to snuggle down in bed and fall asleep.

The last thing he thought about was Simon. Joel would have to go to see him tomorrow, to find out how he was. And who would feed the dogs if Simon couldn't? And the cock in the cabin of the truck?

It had stopped snowing by morning. Reserve goalkeeper Nilsson, who had been driving his snowplow all night, called in at Simon's cottage to feed the dogs. When he got there, the dogs ran off. Nilsson followed them. He found them deep in the forest, keeping guard over Simon's hat. It slowly began to dawn on Nilsson what must have happened.

Had that Gustafson boy really managed to drag Simon all the way from here to the cottage, he wondered.

I doubt if I could have done that, he thought. In a storm like the one we had yesterday.

He drove back to town and sat down to drink coffee

with the rest of his colleagues who had been working all night.

He told them all what must have happened.

Simon was in the hospital. It was obvious to the doctor that he'd had a cerebral hemorrhage. It was too early to say if he would survive or not.

And Joel slept. As it was Sunday, he didn't need to think about going to school.

The mouse gnawed away softly next to his ear.

— SEVENTEEN —

It had never happened before.

That Miss Nederström had been round to Joel's house to see him. But the following day, a Sunday, when Joel was still asleep in bed, there was a knock on the door. Samuel was sitting at the kitchen table, patching a pair of pants. He knew who Miss Nederström was because he had seen her at end-of-term meetings.

"What has Joel done now?" he asked in horror when he opened the door and saw who it was.

"Is he in?" asked Miss Nederström.

"He's asleep," said Samuel. "He must have come home pretty late last night. He spends too much time gallivanting about when he should be in bed. I keep telling him. But it's beyond me, what he was doing out in that storm."

Miss Nederström had come into the kitchen.

"So you haven't yet spoken to your son, Mr. Gustafson?"

"I'll wake him up right away," said Samuel, trying to appear angry with Joel.

She put her hand on his shoulder.

"Don't wake him up. He needs to sleep. I think I can fill you in on what happened."

They sat down at the kitchen table. Miss Nederström accepted the offer of a cup of coffee.

Then she told Samuel what had happened the previous day. How Joel had dragged Simon Windstorm a couple of miles through the raging storm. And how he had then gone to fetch help.

"Mr. Windstorm is seriously ill," said Miss Nederström. "But for Joel, he'd have been dead."

Samuel had listened in astonishment to what she had said. He wasn't sure that he understood everything, but it was clear that for once, Joel hadn't been stirring up trouble.

"Maybe I ought to wake him up," Samuel said.

"No, let him sleep. He must be absolutely exhausted."

They both peeped cautiously round the door to Joel's room. He was lying with his eyes closed and the quilt up to his chin.

They tiptoed quietly back to the kitchen table.

What they hadn't noticed was that Joel was awake. He had screwed up his eyes and seen them as two blurred shadows in the doorway. He had realized that it was Miss Nederström and Samuel. When they went back to the kitchen he sneaked up to the door and listened. He gathered she had come to ask how he was. Not to tell Samuel how difficult he was being at school, when he was there.

"Joel learns things so easily," she said. "But he's careless. And he has so many other things buzzing round in his head."

"It's not always so easy for me to take proper care of him when I'm on my own," said Samuel. "But I do the best I can."

Miss Nederström left shortly afterwards. Joel had managed to hasten back to bed.

He heard her walking down the stairs.

Samuel came to Joel's room. He pretended to be asleep again, but he couldn't fool Samuel.

"I heard you standing behind the door, listening," he said.

He sat down on the edge of Joel's bed.

"What's all this that I ought to know about?" he said. "I want to hear it from you now. How are you feeling?"

"Fine."

"You must be tired out?"

"Not any longer."

Then Joel told his dad what had happened. Samuel listened without saying a word.

"Simon was heavy," said Joel to finish off with. "I didn't think it was possible for a person to weigh as much as that."

Samuel stroked him lightly over the forehead.

"It was as if you'd saved a shipwrecked sailor," he said. "A man overboard, but in the snow. There were enormous breakers in the sea of snow. The gale was howling. But you managed to get him to the shore. Alive.".

Joel understood what Samuel meant. Even though he had never rescued anybody from the real sea.

"It was like swallowing a lot of freezing cold water," he said. "All that snow blowing into my face."

Samuel sat looking at him for ages. Joel liked being looked at by his father.

"Come and lie down in my bed," said Samuel eventually. "We can read a bit of *Mutiny on the Bounty*."

Joel jumped eagerly out of bed. He was aching all over. But it was a long time since he and Samuel had read a book together. Far too long.

Samuel pulled the quilt up to both their chins. Joel felt as if he were hibernating together with a grizzly bear.

"I stood waiting for you outside the shoe shop," Samuel said. "I don't mind telling you I got pretty angry."

"Maybe we can buy the boots next Saturday instead," said Joel.

"You can buy them yourself," Samuel said. "I'll give you the money. It occurs to me that you don't need me with you when you're buying new shoes. Unless I'm much mistaken, you're starting to be grown up."

"I've been grown up for ages," said Joel. "It's just that you haven't noticed until now."

Samuel nodded.

"Maybe I haven't wanted to notice," he said. "You see, if you grow older, so do I. And I don't want to. I think I'm old enough as it is."

Joel suspected that Samuel disliked talking about growing old. Samuel took hold of the book.

"Shall we start at the beginning?" he asked.

"You can choose," said Joel.

"Then we'll read the end first," said Samuel. "That's the best bit."

Then he read about the mysterious island that had suddenly appeared on the horizon. When the mutineers had started mutinying against one another. When Fletcher had hardly been able to control them any longer. The island rose out of the water like a gigantic rock. They had beached the *Bounty* in the shallows and gone ashore.

It was like entering paradise.

And they were still there now. After many hundreds of years.

Samuel closed the book and dropped it onto his stomach.

Both of them lay there in silence.

The wind was howling outside the window, but Joel could hear that the storm was beginning to ease off.

The walls of the house were creaking and crackling. It was like being on board ship. As if they were tossing about on the sea somewhere, in the captain's cabin.

"I'd like to go there," said Joel. "To Pitcairn Island."

"So would I," said Samuel. "To Pitcairn Island."

That was all they said. Joel dozed off and slept for another hour.

Late in the afternoon Joel went to the hospital to visit Simon. Samuel went with him. Joel had promised to show Samuel afterwards where he had found Simon. It had also occurred to Samuel that somebody ought to feed Simon's dogs.

"He keeps hens as well," said Joel. "And a cock that lives in his truck. And perches on the steering wheel."

The snowstorm was over now. Snowplows were still driving round in the streets. The snowdrifts were deep.

When they came to the hospital they were told that they couldn't see Simon. He was still asleep. And he was very ill. They waited until a doctor came out to speak to them. Joel recognized him immediately. He was the one who had looked after Joel when he'd almost been killed by that bus. But the doctor didn't recognize Joel.

"So you were the one who found him, were you?" he said, ruffling Joel's hair.

Joel didn't like his hair being ruffled. Not even by a doctor.

"That was very well done," he said. "A heroic feat."

Then he turned serious.

"But I'm afraid it's not clear what the outcome will

be," he said. "He's had a cerebral hemorrhage. And Windstorm is an old man. It's too soon to say if he's going to make it."

Joel was quiet when they left the hospital. Samuel noticed.

"He might pull through," he said. "Let's hope so, at any rate."

"It wouldn't be fair if he were to die," said Joel.

"Death is never fair, I suppose," said Samuel. "And no matter when death comes, it always makes a mess of everything."

They continued to Simon's house in the trees. The dogs were waiting outside the house. They whimpered when Samuel fed them. Then Joel and Samuel tracked down the four terrified hens and the cockerel. They were huddled together at the very back of the woodshed.

Then Joel and his dad set off into the forest. Joel wasn't absolutely sure where he'd found Simon, but he found the right spot in the end.

Samuel shook his head.

"It's nearly two miles," he said. "How on earth did you manage to drag him all that way back to the house?"

"I just had to," said Joel uncertainly.

He couldn't understand himself how he'd done it.

When they got back to Simon's house, Joel wanted to take the two dogs home with them, and look after them for as long as Simon was ill. But Samuel said no. They belonged to Simon's house. That was where they should stay, nowhere else. But Joel would have to feed them every day.

On their way back through the little town they paused at the shoe shop. Joel pointed out the boots he wanted. Samuel turned pale when he saw the price. But he didn't say anything.

Samuel made dinner that evening. Joel would have preferred to do it himself, because it was hardly ever up to much when Samuel did the cooking. But Samuel could be stubborn. He had decided that Joel needed a rest. While Samuel worked, Joel lay on his bed and thought about all the things that had happened over the last few days. He even brought himself to think about the Greyhound and her laughing friends. It seemed to be easier now that he had dragged Simon through the raging sea of snow. He still worried about going back to school the following day, but he knew he was going to go, no matter what.

Samuel had fried some pork and potatoes. Joel carefully scraped away all the burnt fat.

"Was it good?" Samuel asked.

"Yes," said Joel. "The best I've ever eaten."

But he sighed quietly to himself when Samuel served him another helping.

Grown-ups sometimes had difficulty in understanding what other people really meant.

They went to bed early, Samuel and Joel, that evening.

And Joel slept.

The fried pork was slowly digested in his stomach. Samuel snored, and the mouse gnawed away inside the wall.

Joel had a dream.

He was crossing over the empty street with Wyatt Earp and his brother. Shuffling and coughing behind them was Doc Holliday. The red dust whirled around their feet. Their spurs jingled as they walked.

It was time now. Time to confront Ike Clanton and his gang. They were going to fight a duel at the OK Corral. A few minutes from now a lot of people would be dead. Joel was walking just behind Wyatt Earp. He was wearing boots with spurs. He was in front of Doc Holliday, who was coughing drily. He would soon die. Of tuberculosis. But first they needed to sort out Ike Clanton. They couldn't wait any longer. The moment had come. They could see Ike and his men approaching. Through the heat haze. The sun was turning the air into fog. Then Joel noticed that the Greyhound was there as well. And Ike Clanton's men roared with laughter. Wyatt Earp stopped dead. Everybody stopped. Suddenly they had all vanished. Joel was standing there on his own. He was gripped by panic. The sun was shining straight into his eyes.

He couldn't see a thing. He groped for the pistol that ought to be at his hip. A Smith & Wesson, with the wooden butt removed and replaced by one made of pure silver. But there was nothing there. His holster was empty. Outside the saloon sat Miss Nederström in a creaking rocking chair, fast asleep.

Joel was so scared that his body was screaming inwardly. The Greyhound started running towards him. She grew bigger and bigger, like a giant bird with flapping wings.

He sat up with a shriek. It was dark in the room. At first he didn't know where he was. Then he saw the gleaming pointers of his alarm clock. He was back home again. It had only been a dream. A sling that had fired him to the OK Corral and back.

It was a long time before he could get back to sleep. The dream had been a warning. He would have to go back to school, and that would be like approaching the OK Corral. Without Wyatt Earp. And without Doc Holliday and his tubercular cough.

But when he arrived at the school playground, nothing was as he'd been expecting. The Greyhound was there. And all the rest of them.

But nobody giggled. Nobody pointed.

Nobody pursed their lips or put their head on one side.

Joel realized he had Simon to thank for that. When he entered the classroom he was still unsure of what would happen. But the Greyhound looked guilty. And Miss

197

Nederström started talking even before she played the morning hymn.

She told the whole class what had happened. Joel thought it sounded like an adventure tale. Had he really been the one who had dragged Simon all that way? Or had he dreamt that as well?

Everybody seemed to know about it already. Joel started to wonder if this is how he would be remembered in 2045. The man who once dragged Simon Windstorm through a raging sea of snow.

He thought about Simon Windstorm. Who had a cerebral hemorrhage. And the dogs whining outside his front door.

When the first break came he plucked up courage and asked Miss Nederström what a cerebral hemorrhage was.

"Something that bursts inside your head," she said. "But don't think about that, Joel."

"What else is there for me to think about?" he asked.

Miss Nederström said nothing. And the break was soon over.

After school Joel went straight to the shoe shop. He tried on the new boots. They didn't chafe his ankles. He paid, and was given the old boots back in a cardboard box. Then he hurried up the hill towards the hospital as fast as he could. In his satchel he had a few bones Samuel had given him that morning. He hesitated over what to do first—visit Simon or feed the dogs. It was a hard decision to make. But the dogs were bound to be pleased to see him, and so he started with them.

This time they came running towards him. Joel sat stroking them for a while before looking for the hens. They were all in the truck today. Joel crumbled up some dry bread and put it inside the truck for them.

Then he couldn't wait any longer. He would have to visit Simon. He had a stroke of luck when he got to the hospital, and bumped straight into the doctor he and Samuel had spoken to the day before.

No change. Simon was still unconscious.

Nobody could say if he was going to live or die.

Joel had tears in his eyes. Not because he wanted to. Why should Simon die now that he was in hospital instead of lying in a snowdrift?

Joel left the hospital.

He noticed her immediately.

The Greyhound. She was standing outside the hospital gate.

And she looked nothing like a gigantic bird with flapping, threatening wings.

— EIGHTEEN —

Joel tried to be angry. But he didn't succeed.

They walked down the hill from the hospital. The Greyhound didn't say a word. Nor did she run round and round him like she usually did.

Instead of being angry Joel tried to demonstrate that he couldn't care less about her company. To act as if she weren't there. But that didn't really work either. He would never be an actor.

In the end he decided to be himself and do exactly what he wanted to do. They had come as far as the railway station now.

There were several large snowdrifts just behind the long, red wooden building that housed the freight office. Anybody walking past would think they were only playing.

As they passed the biggest of the snowdrifts Joel tripped the Greyhound up so that she fell backwards into the snow. Then he jumped on top of her and started rubbing snow into her face. She struggled as hard as she could, but Joel was stronger. Then he started to poke snow down inside her clothes. She kicked and scratched and fought back. Joel still wasn't angry, but even so, he had to do what he was doing.

"Stop it!" she shouted.

"Purse your lips," said Joel.

Then he pushed her head into the snow again.

He didn't stop until she had started crying.

"So, now I've gotten you back," he said, standing up.

Her jacket was torn. She was crying as she walked away. Joel thought it was odd that she didn't run. Now, if ever, was the time when she ought to be running.

He set off for home. But suddenly he stopped dead and started following the Greyhound. Now he was the one running, not her.

He caught up with her at the tumbledown old building used as a warehouse by Thulin the ironmonger's. She was still crying, but Joel could tell that it was ebbing out. He walked beside her for quite a while without speaking.

In the end he couldn't keep quiet any longer.

"It served you right," he said. "But I won't do it again."

"Nor will I," she said. "But it wasn't my idea."

Joel stopped dead. What she said couldn't be true.

"I thought you and I were the only ones who knew about it."

"Nearly," she said. "But it wasn't me who wanted to do it even so."

"Who was it, then?"

"The others."

"But you could have told me."

"I wish I had done."

Joel gazed down at the ground. Should he believe her or not?

There was only one way of finding out.

"Show me," he said. "Here and now. How to kiss. Then I'll believe what you say."

"Not out here in the street," she said.

"We can go behind this building. Nobody lives here. There's only saws and axes and such stuff inside."

"Another time."

"In that case, I don't believe you."

She looked at him angrily.

"But I've been crying! I can't stand here kissing somebody when I've been crying! Don't you understand anything?"

Joel felt unsure.

"I'll wait, then," he said.

"I have to go home now," said the Greyhound. "I'll be in trouble if I don't."

"When shall we do it, then? If I'm going to believe you?"

"Later," she said. "I promise."

And now she started running. Joel felt relieved that they hadn't stopped being friends despite everything. He still felt he couldn't trust her completely, but he felt better even so. And he'd gotten her back.

Joel went to the railway station. Checked to see if anybody had dropped any small change behind the wooden benches. An old man was sitting with his back resting against the wall, fast asleep. Stationmaster Knif was shouting inside the ticket office, telling somebody off. Joel paused in front of the big timetable pinned to the wall. Somebody had crossed out the name of the little town and written in pencil:

No trains stop here. Only idiots stop in this dump.

Joel giggled. He wondered if Knif had seen that. How would he have reacted, in that case? He must have been raving mad.

The old man asleep by the wall was snoring. It seemed to Joel that he must be a hundred years old. Which would mean he'd been born in 1858. At about the same time as Wyatt Earp and Doc Holliday had walked down that deserted street for the showdown with Ike Clanton and his gang.

Joel sat down on a bench and dangled his feet. That was another problem when it came to having parents, he thought. You can't choose yourself what time you want to live in.

Joel knew of course that this was a silly way of thinking. Childish. But good fun even so.

If he could have chosen, he'd have been one of Fletcher's right-hand men. The one who would take over from Fletcher eventually. And then he wouldn't have needed to sit around in a boring railway station with an old man fast asleep.

He'd have been in a totally different world.

In that world the leaves of palm trees rustled in the wind and women walked around in transparent veils.

Now he was back on that subject again! He stood up in annoyance. Stamped his feet hard to see if he could wake up the old man. Not a chance.

He checked his watch. Too late. Ehnström's had closed. And he couldn't very well just march up and ring her doorbell. Not when he didn't have any Christmas magazines to sell, nor any mittens to look for. Besides, that unknown man might be there. The one who'd been holding hands with her at the cinema. It could be risky if he was. He might throw Joel out. Even out of the window. The man might be wild with jealousy. You could never tell in advance.

He started pedaling with his feet. Lumps of slush and dirt dripped off his boots and onto the floor. They looked as if they'd formed a map. An archipelago of islands. He started giving names to the various stains. "Snake Island," "Doc Holliday's Skerry," "Windstorm Rocks."

But all the time what he was really thinking about was Sonja Mattsson.

He wondered if he would ever see her wearing transparent veils.

Joel looked at the old man. And decided to get some help from fate. If he succeeded in waking the old man up before anybody else came into the waiting room, he would see Sonja Mattsson in transparent veils. He wasn't allowed to shake the old man. Nor to shout. But everything else was permitted.

If the old man was still asleep the next time the waiting-room door opened, he could forget all about that business of the transparent veils. Fate would have made its decision.

Joel started kicking one of the bench legs, which were made of steel. All the time he was keeping an eye on the ticket office window. It could open at any moment. Knif had ears that could pick up the sound of a train fifty miles away. But the old man didn't wake up. Joel kicked even harder. The old man snored. Joel was really furious with him by now. Maybe he was dead? Joel stood up and took hold of the backrest of the bench the old man was sitting on. He started shaking it. The old man grunted and rubbed at his nose. But he didn't wake up. Joel shook so hard that the whole bench started jumping up and down. No effect. He was sure the waiting-room door would open at any moment now. He thought desperately about what he could do. Then he hit on the only possible solution. He ran to the ticket office window, which was closed, and hammered on it as hard as he could. It opened immediately. Stationmaster Knif was staring Joel in the face.

"What do you want, belting on the window like that?" he roared. "Do you want a ticket?"

"I was just checking if you were awake," said Joel with a grin.

Knif turned red in the face.

"Get out!" he bellowed. "Get out of here!'

It echoed all round the waiting room.

And the old man woke up.

Joel ran off before Knif could come storming into the room—but the old man had woken up! That was the important thing. Knif's voice could awaken the dead.

So fate had decided. Joel would get to see Sonja Mattsson wearing nothing but transparent veils.

He hurried home as fast as he could. No doubt Samuel would have made dinner and be wondering why Joel hadn't come home.

Joel could imagine how astonished Samuel would be, if he heard what fate had decided.

One evening very soon I, Joel Gustafson, will visit the flat of Sonja Mattsson, also known as Salome, and see her naked behind transparent veils.

Samuel would doubtless fall down in a faint on the cork floor tiles.

Joel also wondered if Samuel had seen Sara wearing

transparent veils. Now that would have been a sight for sore eyes.

But needless to say, when Joel got home he didn't say anything about what fate had ordained.

And Samuel hadn't finished making dinner. Typical! He was always messing about and never finished anything in time.

He had been a sailor. And he was a lumberjack. But Joel didn't think his father was up to much as a cook.

The next day the Greyhound and Joel wrote a never-ending stream of notes to each other. By the end of the school day Joel's pocket was full of them. They were friends again, it seemed. None of the others who had been present when Joel sat on that chair and pursed his lips said a word. They didn't even smirk. Even Otto evidently felt obliged to be nice to Joel. It wasn't just any old boy who was capable of dragging Simon Windstorm goodness knows how many miles through the snow.

During one of the breaks Otto wanted to show Joel one of the secret magazines he'd acquired.

"It's a new one," he said. "Nobody else has seen the pictures yet."

"I think I'll give it a miss," Joel said. "The real thing is more exciting."

Otto stared at him. Joel stared back. Otto daren't say that Joel was just making it up.

It was a good day. One of the best for a very long time.

After school Joel fed the dogs and the chickens at Simon's place. The Greyhound went with him. Joel let her feed the chickens while he dealt with the dogs. Then they heard from the hospital that there was no change in Simon's condition. He was still seriously ill.

Joel felt sad. The Greyhound tried to console him.

"At least he's no worse," she said. "That has to be good news."

Joel could see that she was right. It was good not to have to do all the thinking yourself. The Greyhound was good company. Even if she was a girl.

They said goodbye outside her front door. She hadn't said anything about kissing. Nor had Joel asked.

Once the Greyhound had vanished into the block of flats, it occurred to Joel that he ought to tell Kringström that he would soon be calling round again for a lesson. But then he saw that the black van used by the orchestra wasn't there. So Kringström wasn't at home.

Joel went straight to Ehnström's grocery store. He needed to buy a lot of things today. The bell rang as he opened the door, and he saw that it was Sonja behind the counter. Joel took off his hat and gave his hair a quick stroke. He'd forgotten to do that before entering the shop. There were lots of old ladies to be served before him. She still hadn't noticed that he was there. He was able to watch her surreptitiously. Once again he imagined her in transparent veils. But that wasn't easy, not with all the other women jostling one another in the shop. He would have to think them away. He tried to imagine that he was alone in the shop. But he couldn't. It just wasn't right, her moving back and forth behind the counter and weighing flour. And then she noticed him. Joel gave a jump, as if she had been able to read his thoughts.

"I think it's your turn now," she said.

All the old ladies started muttering and moaning, but Joel took the opportunity of marching up to the counter. It was about time he had the upper hand. Those ladies had so often elbowed their way in front of him in line.

"How's your brother?" she asked. "How's Digby?"

Joel wished the floor would swallow him up.

Needless to say, one of the old ladies couldn't resist putting her oar in.

"He doesn't have a brother," she said.

Joel didn't know where he got the courage from, but he just turned round and looked the woman in the eye.

"It's funny how some people just can't resist butting in on other people's conversation," he said.

Then he turned to look at Sonja.

"Digby's fine," he said. "His knee and his shoulder are both OK. I'd like some eggs and some butter, please."

The old lady said nothing. Sonja collected what he'd asked for.

"I heard that you rescued somebody who was in danger of freezing to death in the forest," she said.

She spoke loudly so that everybody could hear. Joel was impressed.

"He was heavy," Joel said. "But anything's possible if you put your mind to it."

She worked out what he owed and wrote it down in a book. Samuel called in and paid once a month. Joel initialed the amount.

"Why not come round to my place and tell me all about it?" she said.

Joel couldn't believe his ears. Neither could all the old ladies. This new shop assistant from Stockholm was actually inviting Joel to pop round and visit her?

"When?" Joel asked.

"Why not this evening?" she said.

Joel collected his carrier bags and left. Nobody jostled him.

When he emerged into the street he found it necessary to put down his bags. Had he heard right?

Then he realized he was short of time. If he was going to call round and visit her tonight, he needed time to get himself ready.

Joel thought about the man in the waiting room.

It certainly was lucky that he'd managed to wake the old codger up.

*　*　*

When Joel got home he started making dinner straight-away. Samuel would be back from the forest any minute now. As he worked, Joel found himself thinking all the time about what was going to happen later that evening. He was so confused that it was ages before he realized that he'd forgotten to switch on the pan with the potatoes. Every other minute he went to check his face in the mirror. He used water in an effort to make his close-cropped hair stand up as it should. But he couldn't do anything about the cowlick over his forehead.

Even if he lived to be a hundred years old, it would still be there.

He could hear Samuel's footsteps on the stairs. Like an elephant. He was coming into the kitchen now.

He's going to say that it smells good, Joel thought.

"That smells good," Samuel said. "How's Simon? Have you fed his dogs?"

Joel told him what the situation was. No change as far as Simon was concerned. And the dogs had been fed.

They had dinner. Joel wolfed his down. Samuel looked at him in surprise.

"I'm going out," Joel said.

"Again?"

"We have to prepare the school Christmas party. Even if Christmas does seem to be a long way away yet."

Samuel nodded. Then he sighed.

"Time flies," Samuel said.

"You have to try to keep abreast of it," Joel said. And wondered what on earth he'd meant by that.

Shortly after seven o'clock he was standing outside her flat. He'd run the whole way. Now he was getting his breath back.

He entered the front door again.

He was quite certain now.

This evening she would welcome him dressed in nothing but transparent veils.

— NINETEEN —

Sonja Mattsson opened the door.

But she was not dressed in transparent veils. She had rollers in her hair. Just like the ones Joel had seen in Sara's hair. He couldn't help pulling a face. He'd been so sure she would open the door wearing nothing apart from transparent veils.

"Have you never seen rollers before?" she asked.

Joel blushed. She had seen through him.

"Yes, I have," he said. "But not on you."

She looked at him in surprise.

"What had you expected?"

Joel gave a start. *She had read his thoughts.* He waited for what was coming next. No doubt she would box his ears and throw him out. She might go to the local newspaper and tell the editor. Next week everybody would be able to read about it.

Joel Gustafson thinks forbidden thoughts.

The veil man Joel Gustafson still at large.

"How much longer are you going to stand there gaping?" she asked. "It's drafty."

Joel stepped into the hall.

"Hang your jacket up and come in. But take your boots off first."

This time he didn't hide a mitten or his scarf. He followed her into the living room. She had sat down and tucked her feet up. She was wearing a pink dressing gown. He could see a bit of one thigh, but he didn't dare to look properly.

She nodded at his feet.

"No holes in your socks," she said.

"My mum has darned them," said Joel.

She had lit a cigarette, and looked thoughtful as she blew a few rings.

"People talk a lot in this dump," she said.

"Yes, you can't have any secrets here."

"People talk," she said again. "About this and that. When you serve in a shop you get to hear all kinds of interesting things. Do you know what I heard today? After you'd left?"

Joel shook his head.

"That what that old lady said was true. That you don't

have a brother called Digby. You don't have a brother at all, in fact."

She didn't seem angry when she said that. She was smiling. A friendly smile. Joel realized that he had no choice but to tell her the truth.

"I wanted to sell you some Christmas magazines," he mumbled. "So I was forced to invent Digby."

Joel told her about Otto. About having to pay him three kronor. She burst out laughing. But she still didn't seem angry.

"Everybody's talking about Joel Gustafson," she said when it became obvious that Joel wasn't going to say any more about the magazines.

"Nothing they say is true," said Joel.

"Oh, the odd grain of truth comes out," she said. "But I agree that the old ladies come out with lots of things they haven't a clue about."

"This dump is full of gossips," said Joel. "You can't even piss in the snow without everybody getting to hear about it."

She laughed again.

"Just now, everybody's talking about you," she said. "Everybody thinks it was terrific of you to save the life of that old man."

"Simon Windstorm," said Joel. "That's his name."

"Windstorm?"

"Yes, Windstorm."

"I wish I'd been called that," she said. "It sounds better than Mattsson."

"It sounds better than Gustafson as well."

"People talk," she said again. "Today somebody told me you didn't have a brother. But they also said that you don't have a mother."

I'm off, Joel thought. She knows everything. She'll soon come out with the veils business. She can read thoughts. She doesn't just listen to gossipy old women.

"It's none of my business, of course," she said. "But obviously, I wonder who it is that does darn your wooly socks."

"I do it myself," said Joel. "I do all the shopping and the cooking. I'm my own mum. But that means I don't have to put up with somebody nagging at me all the time. If I want there to be some nagging, I do it myself."

She suddenly looked serious.

"I'm only asking because I'm curious," she said. "That's one of my big faults. I'm much too curious."

"So am I," said Joel. "But I don't think it's a fault."

She stubbed out her cigarette. Joel looked at her red lips. He could feel his passions stirring. What if those lips could teach him how to kiss? That would be a bit different from the Greyhound doing it.

"I've made tea," she said, rising to her feet. "Would you like some?"

"Yes, please," said Joel.

He hated tea. All it did was make him want to pee. But

216

this was Sonja Mattsson offering him tea. So he couldn't possibly say no.

She came back with two cups and a teapot. Joel tasted it. It tasted awful, but he drank it even so.

"Tell me what happened," she said. "Out there in the snow."

Joel told her the facts. How he had found Simon and dragged him back to the house. As she seemed to be able to check absolutely everything, he didn't dare to exaggerate. Although he would have liked to do, of course.

"You must be strong," she said. "And persistent."

"Oh, I don't know," said Joel. "You just do the best you can."

She put down her cup and lit another cigarette.

"Do you smoke?" she asked.

Joel was on the point of saying he did, but managed to stop himself in time. If he lit a cigarette he would start coughing immediately.

He shook his head. He didn't want a cigarette.

"Now you can ask me," she said. "Only two questions. No more."

Joel thought. Two questions were not many. He would have to be careful. What did he want to know most?

"Why have you come here?" he asked.

That was what he wanted to know more than anything else. How could somebody who lived in Stockholm choose of their own free will to move to a dump like this?

"I needed to get away," she said. "Things got a bit too much for me."

Joel noticed that she had changed. Her face was much more serious now.

He wondered if he'd asked something inappropriate.

"There were too many men," she went on. "And some of them wouldn't leave me alone. That's why I came here. I don't know how long I'll stay. We'll have to see. How I get on. How I feel. What happens. And if I can stand the long winter."

Joel tried to work out the significance of what she'd said. Too many men? What did she mean by that? And that they wouldn't leave her alone?

There was no doubt about what the next question would have to be. Joel didn't need to hesitate. He was curious and he couldn't deny that he was jealous.

"Who were you with at the cinema the other night?"

She sat there with her teacup halfway to her mouth.

"How do you know I was at the cinema?"

"I was there," said Joel. "But the film wasn't very good."

"It was adults only," she said. "And you're not fifteen yet."

"I get in through a secret door," said Joel.

She put her cup down.

"Now you're telling me lies," she said.

She seemed angry for the first time.

"It's true," said Joel.

"How did the film end?" she asked abruptly.

"I don't know."

"There you are! You're lying!'

"I had to leave just before the end. If I hadn't, Engman would notice that I'd sneaked in. If I'd still been there when the lights went up."

"Who's Engman?"

"The caretaker who runs the place."

"I still don't believe you. You weren't there."

"I can tell you what happened when there were only five minutes left."

The words came pouring out of his mouth. He talked and talked until she believed him. He retold the story of the film back to front. He told her about the door in the basement. The only thing he didn't mention was the Greyhound.

She had started smiling again. She believed him.

"OK, we were both at the cinema," she said. "And you want to know who I was with?"

"Who were you sitting next to, holding hands?"

Joel heard to his surprise that he sounded angry. And she had noticed.

"That will have to be my secret," she said. "I let him hold my hand, but that's all."

"You didn't put any veils on for him?"

Joel almost bit his tongue off. But it was too late. He couldn't pull the words back into his mouth. They weren't on strings. Joel had often thought how useful it would be, when he'd said something he regretted, if he could haul the words back in.

She looked at him in astonishment.

"What do you mean by that?" she asked.

"Nothing," said Joel, quickly.

He could see that he'd set her thinking.

"You gave Otto three kronor so that you could sell me a magazine," she said slowly. "And I think you left that mitten behind on purpose. You sounded almost angry when you told me that you'd seen me at the cinema with somebody who was holding my hand. And you even invented a brother who doesn't exist. Why?"

Joel could feel himself blushing. He stared down at the floor.

"I don't bite," she said. "I neither sting nor scratch. Unless I want to. And I don't want to just now. Come on, what did you say?"

Her voice sounded gentle now. Joel almost dared to look at her.

"I don't gossip," she said. "It will stay within these four walls. Just between you and me. Cross my heart."

Joel looked up at her.

"Cross my heart," she said again. "Cross my heart."

Joel didn't dare. But he said it even so. He thought he would drop down dead on the spot.

"I thought you'd be wearing transparent veils when you opened the door. Nothing else."

He said it very quietly. And very fast. But she heard.

"Why did you want that to happen? And why me?"

"I don't know. But it was going to be a secret."

She leaned back in her chair and looked at him. Joel hardly dared to meet her eye. He hoped she wasn't going to throw him out the window. That she'd let him leave through the door.

He said as much.

"My dad, Samuel, would appreciate it if I got back home alive. I'm going now."

He started to stand up.

"You have time for another cup of tea," she said. "I'll just boil some more water."

She took the teapot with her into the kitchen. Joel noticed that he was covered in sweat. Maybe he ought to take this opportunity to sneak out. She wouldn't be able to see the hall from the kitchen.

But he stayed on the chair. Heard the clattering noises in the kitchen. Then everything went quiet. He waited.

All of a sudden, there she was. In the kitchen doorway. And she was naked. Apart from something very thin, a net curtain perhaps. Or a veil. Joel stared.

Then she disappeared.

She came back into the room a couple of minutes later. Now she was wearing the pink dressing gown again. And carrying the teapot.

"I saw you," Joel said.

She looked surprised.

"Saw what?"

"The veils."

She frowned.

"Are you suggesting I stood here wearing veils?"

"In the kitchen doorway."

"You must have been dreaming."

Joel thought for a moment. He realized that she was creating a secret that they could share. There was no better way of protecting a secret than claiming that what happened was really just a dream.

"Yes," said Joel. "I suppose it was just a dream."

"That will never come back," she said. "Remember that."

She said it with a smile. But firmly.

"No, I don't suppose it will ever come back," said Joel. "You only have dreams like that once."

They sat drinking their tea in silence.

"You'd better go home now," she said. "It's late and I need to get some sleep."

Joel put on his boots and jacket in the hall. She stood in the doorway, watching him.

"Thank you for the dream," he said when he was ready to go.

"It was nothing much," she said. "It was so little that it was almost nothing at all."

When Joel emerged into the street he turned round. She was standing in the window. When he waved, she waved back.

He walked home through the dark. It was a starry night, and cold. He felt as if he were in a church.

The whole world was a church.

The street home was an aisle between rows of invisible pews.

He had seen her naked. Just for a second. Or maybe two. But he knew now. It wasn't like the pictures in Otto's magazines. Or at least, not only like that. There was more to it than that.

Several times he was forced to pause. Breathe in, breathe out, breathe in again.

Then he started running.

If the Greyhound had been there, he would have been able to catch up with her for the first and perhaps the only time.

He felt he simply had to tell somebody about it. Despite the fact that he wasn't allowed to. He'd promised.

Then he stopped dead. There was one person, he thought, who was guaranteed not to gossip. He turned off into a different street, and started running again.

He was less frightened this time. The churchyard didn't seem so threatening. He stood in front of Lars Olson's headstone. Where he had made his New Year's resolutions. He could announce that one of his resolutions had come true already.

"I've seen a naked woman," he said. "Sonja Mattsson."

The headstone said nothing.

"I want Simon to be fit again," he muttered. "I don't want him to die."

He didn't get an answer. But then, he hadn't expected one.

He set off running again. He was on his way home now. Samuel would be sitting with the wireless on, waiting for him. Or perhaps he would have gone to bed and be asleep already?

But when he entered the kitchen, the black avalanche engulfed him again.

Samuel wasn't at home. He had vanished.

Joel slumped onto a chair and howled out loud. It sounded like a foghorn.

He didn't have any strength left. Samuel could drink himself to death, if that was what he wanted.

But surely that wasn't what he wanted? Joel was convinced of that. All the time Samuel kept on doing things he didn't want to do.

There was a half-empty cup of coffee on the table. Joel dipped a finger into it.

The coffee was still warm.

Joel jumped to his feet.

That meant Samuel couldn't have been away for long.

Maybe Joel would be able to catch him before he started drinking.

Joel grabbed his wooly hat.

And went out again.

— TWENTY —

Joel stood motionless in the street. Holding his breath. He looked slowly in both directions. No sign of Samuel. The starry sky up above was no longer visible. Clouds had come creeping in from nowhere. Perhaps it would start snowing again.

But the stars couldn't help him to find Samuel in any case. He would have to find his own way to wherever he was. Without the Plow or Orion as navigational aids.

Joel racked his brains.

Samuel seldom returned to the same drinking den several times in a row. So Joel could exclude the ramshackle house by the river where the Crow and the Goblin brothers generally sat drinking.

Joel was thinking as fast as he could. It would be best

if he could catch Samuel before he'd got to wherever he was heading. But where would that be?

That lonely foghorn was still howling inside him.

I'll give him a good thumping, he thought bitterly. I'll give Samuel a punch on the nose. Knock him over.

If I had the strength to drag Simon home through the snow, I'll be up to doing the same with Samuel. And then I'll tie him down to his bed.

Joel started walking towards the western edge of town. There were two places in that direction that Samuel could be heading. He walked slowly at first, then faster and faster. When Samuel got it into his head that he fancied a drink, he was always in a hurry. It was as if he had a stomach upset and needed to make a dash for the lavatory. Joel couldn't know how big a start his father had on him. A cup of warm coffee wasn't the same as a clock. He walked even faster. The little town was asleep.

There's only me, Joel thought.

Hunting for Samuel. And I've solemnly promised to give him a good thumping when I catch up with him.

Then I'll drag him home.

Or maybe I ought to drag him to the rubbish dump instead? Get rid of the problem once and for all? Then I can take the bus to Ljusdal and continue over the oceans to Pitcairn Island.

He passed by the railway line and sidings, where the

big, dark building containing the abattoir was situated. The streetlights were starting to thin out. Joel hurried on his way. He paused at the crossroads.

Then he saw Samuel. It couldn't be anybody else. He was on his way to the sawmill. There were a few places there where people used to gather to drink. The police had been called out there once or twice, Joel knew that. Somebody had been stabbed in the arm during a fight. There had been an article about it in the newspaper. Samuel had turned very pale when he read about it.

The sight of Samuel on the road made Joel feel a mixture of relief and anger. It meant he had caught him in time. Samuel hadn't yet settled down with a glass or a bottle in his hand.

He started running. The snow creaked under his boots. But Samuel didn't hear him. He didn't notice anything until Joel materialized by his side.

Samuel paused and eyed him up and down. Then continued walking.

"Go home, Joel. Stop following me."

Joel was in front of Samuel now. Walking backwards.

"You said you weren't going to go out drinking anymore. You said that, didn't you?"

Samuel didn't answer. He tried to walk past, but Joel stood in his way. He was angry now. So angry that tears were welling up in his eyes.

"Come home with me now," he said.

"I'll go home soon," said Samuel. "I need a bit of a change. I get so miserable sitting at home on my own."

"Getting drunk won't make things any better."

"I'll have a glass or two whenever it suits me."

Joel felt as if he were talking to a tree. Samuel simply wasn't listening.

He stopped dead. Samuel almost barged into him.

"Come home with me now," said Joel. He was pleading.

"I'll be home soon," said Samuel. "Don't you bother about me."

The words echoed like thunder inside Joel's head. *Don't you bother about me*. Didn't Samuel understand anything at all?

Joel flung himself at his father and started punching him in the chest. The road was slippery. Samuel fell, and dragged Joel down with him. They landed in a snowdrift. Joel could see the Greyhound underneath him. He remembered how he had gotten her back by poking snow inside her clothes.

Why not do the same with Samuel? He started rubbing snow into his father's face. Samuel grunted and growled in surprise. Then he started resisting. But Joel didn't give up. He thrust more and more snow into his father's face and tried to poke some down inside his shirt. He kept going until Samuel grabbed him by his coat collar and flung him to one side.

"What do you think you're doing?" said Samuel, starting to brush the snow off his clothes.

Joel attacked him again. He didn't bother about snow anymore, just hit and punched, and Samuel had to defend himself as best he could.

Then it all stopped. Joel was lying flat on his back in the middle of the road.

Samuel had stood up.

"You can't lie here," he said.

"Oh no?" said Joel. "I can lie here and freeze to death."

Samuel bent down, took hold of Joel's arm and pulled him to his feet. Samuel was strong when he wanted to be.

"I've had enough of all this stupidity," he said. "Go home. And leave me in peace. I'm a grown-up and I'll do as I like."

"If anybody here is grown up, it's me," said Joel. "I don't know what you are."

"How dare you stand here insulting your own father!"

"I'm not insulting anybody. I'm just telling the truth."

Samuel was on edge now. No doubt he was longing for a drink as well. But when he was on edge he could become hot-headed. Joel took a step backwards.

"Go home this minute," said Samuel.

"I'll burn the house down," said Joel.

Samuel was angry. On edge and hot-headed. He tried to grab hold of Joel, who was expecting it and managed to jump out of the way.

"I don't want to hear another word from you," said Samuel. "If you don't go home this very minute, I'll...I don't know what I'll do."

"You can always beat me to death," said Joel. "But who would cook for you then?"

Samuel made another attempt to grab hold of him. They were dancing round each other in the middle of the road.

"Say that again . . . ," said Samuel, threateningly.

Joel shouted it out so loud that it echoed.

"You can always beat me to death. But who would cook for you then?"

"People will hear you," said Samuel. "Stop shouting."

Now he was the one doing the pleading.

"There's nobody around to hear," said Joel.

Then all the wind went out of his sails. He didn't have the strength anymore. He felt like a balloon that had burst.

"Go home this very minute," said Samuel again. "Leave me in peace. I'll be back soon. This is the last time. I promise."

Samuel turned round. Joel saw his hunched back. Watched him walk away, getting smaller and smaller. Until he was swallowed up completely by the darkness.

Joel walked home. His head was completely empty. He had no strength left at all. If this was what life was like, he could do without it. No matter what he did, Samuel spoiled everything for him.

He returned to the house by the river. He'd made up his mind by then. He went up to his room and fetched the mattress and the quilt. Then he dragged the old bed out of the woodshed and placed it in front of the steps up to the front door. When Samuel eventually came home he wouldn't be able to avoid seeing him. No matter how drunk he was.

Joel lay down and pulled the quilt over him. It was cold. But he didn't care anymore. He didn't care about anything at all.

He slowly dozed off. And fell asleep.

Occasional flakes of snow started to drift down onto the bed. Then more. It had begun snowing again. Silently in the night.

Joel had a dream. It was morning and he opened the roller blind. He could even hear the thwacking noise in his dream. The previous night it had been white everywhere when he went to bed. Now everything was different. He stared out the window in surprise. The sea stretched out in front of him. It was blue and green and glinting in the sunlight. Dolphins were jumping in the far distance. The beach was beneath his window. A fishing boat was heading for land. Brown men were paddling through the breakers. The boat was riding on the crest of the waves. In the stern, by the tiller, was somebody he recognized. It was Simon. Pitcairn Island, he thought. So we did get there in the end. Now I'm on Pitcairn Island. And Simon got better and came along with Samuel and me. He opened the window. Then he heard somebody calling his name.

When he opened his eyes he couldn't make out the face in front of him at first. Then he realized it was Samuel. But he didn't care who it was. He wanted to carry on sleeping. To slip back into his dream again. Something seemed to lift him up. He thought it could be a wave. He floated around in the warm water. Perhaps he was riding on one of those dolphins he'd seen not long ago.

He slept deeply. Had no desire to wake up. But there was somebody shaking him. He tried to defend himself. But the shaking continued. In the end he was forced to open his eyes.

Now he could see clearly. It was Samuel's face leaning down over him.

"What on earth do you think you're doing?" said Samuel. "You could have frozen to death down there outside the front door. What would have happened if I hadn't come home when I did?"

Joel started to remember. He noticed that he was lying in Samuel's bed. Down at the foot end he could see the little mat. And he had a hot-water bottle on his stomach. Even so, he felt freezing cold.

He tried to recall what had happened. He'd got into bed, and must have fallen asleep.

He looked at Samuel's face. His eyes were not red. And he didn't smell of strong drink.

"You could have frozen to death," Samuel said again.

"That might have been just as well," said Joel. "Then you wouldn't have had all this trouble."

"You mustn't talk like that," said Samuel.

There was a lively glint in his eye now, Joel could see that.

Joel sat up. He was aching all over.

"Why did you come back?" he asked.

Samuel shook his head.

"I went to where I'd intended going," he said. "But I suddenly had the feeling that I couldn't stay. I didn't know what the matter was. I went home. And there you were in the bed, covered in snow. You could have frozen to death. Can't you understand that? What would have happened if I hadn't come back so soon?"

"Well, what would have happened?" asked Joel.

Samuel didn't answer. He just shook his head.

Joel was tired. He settled down in bed again. He wanted to return to his dream as soon as possible.

And Samuel was there.

He'd come back.

Joel woke up early. He lay in Samuel's bed and tried to remember what had happened. He was wide awake instantly. He recalled that he had gone to sleep in the bed outside the front door. And almost frozen to death. He felt his body underneath the quilt. He wiggled his toes and clenched his fists. So he didn't have frostbite. Then he got up and slipped his feet into Samuel's enormous slippers.

Samuel was in Joel's bed. Joel thought that would probably have been a good thing. To change places with each other once and for all. Then he went to the kitchen. He could see through the window that it had been snowing.

He could see something else as well.

The old bed was still standing there, outside the front door. And it was white. Samuel had left the mattress there. It looked almost as if somebody was lying in the bed, asleep.

Joel felt scared. What had he really done? He could easily have been dead by now. Just as dead as Lars Olson. And just as old. If Samuel hadn't come back when he did.

Samuel had changed his mind. He hadn't started drinking again. That was why it was only the mattress still out there, buried under the snow.

Joel sat down at the kitchen table. Lit a candle. The smell of the wax helped him to calm down.

He'd often thought that his mum, Jenny, was bound to have smelled like a living candle.

It wasn't six yet. Samuel would wake up soon. Joel put the coffee water on the stove. Then he got dressed.

When the coffee was made he could hear that Samuel was moving about. He came into the kitchen.

"Coffee's ready," said Joel.

Samuel looked at him.

"How do you feel?" he asked.

"Fine."

They didn't say any more about it. It wasn't necessary. Samuel and Joel could talk to each other in silence just as well as with words. When they really tried. And this was one of those mornings.

Samuel was dressed, and drinking his coffee.

"Sara's not the only woman around," Joel said. "There are others. And you ought to shave more often."

"I know," said Samuel.

Joel drank a glass of milk.

"We ought to get away from here," Joel said. "There are schools in other places. And there are bound to be forests as well. If you really have to spend the rest of your life chopping down trees."

Samuel looked at him. But he didn't say anything.

"There might be forests on Pitcairn Island," Joel said. "We could write and ask, in any case."

"Do that," said Samuel. "I'll give you the money for a stamp."

"How much is it to send a letter there?" Joel asked. "It's a long way away."

Samuel looked worried.

"We'd better make enquiries at the post office," he said.

Joel had another idea.

"I know what I want for Christmas," he said. "A postage stamp."

"We can't wait that long," said Samuel, standing up.

He placed a five-kronor note on the table next to the burning candle.

"That must surely be enough," he said.

"It's bound to be," said Joel. "The world can't be *that* big."

Samuel left for work. Joel stood in the window and watched him put down his rucksack and carry the bed away. Then he turned round, looked up at the window and waved. Joel waved back.

He started getting ready for school. The Christmas holidays were not far away now. He wondered what kind of a report he would get for this term. The only thing he could be sure about was his mark for geography. What worried him most was what Miss Nederström might decide to give him for general attendance and behavior. No doubt he could expect some unpleasant surprises there.

He blew out the candle. Breathed in the smell. Thought of Mummy Jenny. And Sonja Mattsson.

But most of all he thought of the Greyhound.

Then he left. For once he was in good time for school.

AND TIME CONTINUED
TO RACE PAST. . . .

Christmas was approaching. School had broken up for the holidays. Joel had reluctantly allowed himself to be dressed up as a shepherd when they assembled in the church to listen to the headmaster's boring Christmas address.

Afterwards, Joel had gone home with his school report in his jacket pocket. It hadn't been as bad as he'd feared It might be, although it could have been better. Still, he knew that Samuel would be pleased and proud: Joel was one of the top ten in his class. And he had the highest mark of anybody in geography.

He'd put his report in the middle of the kitchen table.

Then he'd walked to the hospital to visit Simon.

Simon was still poorly, but the doctor told Joel that the chances of his recovering were rather better now. He might even be able to talk.

"Simon never says much," Joel had said. "So it will be enough if he can only talk a little bit."

When Joel left the hospital, the Greyhound was waiting for him outside. They continued up the hill to Simon's house and fed the dogs. They did that every day. Joel had been forced to tell Kringström that he couldn't go to practice the guitar and dust and wash up, not while Simon was ill in hospital. Kringström had heard about what had happened, and said that it was OK for Joel to attend whenever he had time.

Quite a lot had changed. Every time Joel went to do the shopping and Sonja Mattsson was behind the counter, she spent ages talking to him.

The fat old ladies were not very pleased about that. But Sonja told them they could go and do their shopping somewhere else, if they couldn't wait until it was their turn.

Joel and Sonja had a secret they shared. That was nobody else's business.

Samuel hadn't gone off drinking again. Joel could never be certain that his dad wouldn't simply disappear one of these days, but it did seem as if Samuel was now starting to think seriously about moving away from their little town by the river. Perhaps he might even try to become a sailor again, despite everything.

Samuel had finished reading *Mutiny on the Bounty*, and then started it all over again.

Joel had decided to postpone toughening himself up. He wouldn't sleep in the snow again. Not now. Later, perhaps. After all, there was a long time to go until 2045.

He still thought he would be able to become a rock idol. But it had dawned on him that it would probably take rather longer than he'd thought at first. Even learning to play the guitar was pretty difficult. But he was getting better. He knew nine chords now, and the strings didn't dig so deeply into his fingers anymore.

The Greyhound went with Joel to Simon's house every afternoon. They never talked about what had happened that evening in her flat.

Joel waited and waited.

The day that school broke up for Christmas, the Greyhound had accompanied him to Simon's house as usual. She suddenly disappeared while Joel was feeding the dogs.

When she came back, Joel noticed that she had painted her lips red.

They were standing in the middle of Simon's living room.

"Now I'll teach you," she said.

And she did. Joel knew that he would never forget that

feeling as long as he lived. The Greyhound's lips against his.

Afterwards, she giggled.

And Joel blushed.

It was the last Sunday in Advent, the Sunday before Christmas. Joel asked if the Greyhound would like to go with him and watch the night train.

"Is that anything worth watching?" she wondered.

"Maybe somebody will get on and travel away from here," said Joel. "Or maybe somebody will get off. Besides, I need to post a letter."

The Greyhound could be very nosey.

"Who to?"

"Nobody you know."

"To a girl?"

"No."

"Are you sure?"

"I promise."

Lots of people had gathered on the platform when the train arrived. There was a squeaking and clattering as the enormous iron wheels ground to a halt. Stationmaster Knif strutted around, making sure that everything functioned as it ought to do. Joel led the Greyhound to the mail coach. He had the letter in his hand.

"Who's it to?" she asked again.

"I'll tell you another time. But it's not to a girl."

When Knif wasn't looking, Joel popped the letter into the box.

This time he'd attached a real postage stamp.

They remained on the platform, watching the train heading south, towards the railway bridge and the world.

Then they wandered around town, stopping at various shop windows to admire the Christmas decorations.

Joel asked if the Greyhound would like to go with him and pay a visit to Gertrud. She hadn't been there yet. And Joel thought it was a long time since he'd been there himself.

She would love to. But not tonight. It was late already. Her parents would be worried if she didn't go home now.

Joel saw her home.

He watched her disappear through the front door. Looked forward to meeting her the next day again. He needed to practice kissing.

It was cold. The sky was clear and full of stars. Joel stopped between two streetlights and gazed up at the heavens.

He thought about the letter he'd written that was now on its way southwards. Wondered if it would ever reach its destination.

But he was quite sure about the address, in any case.

To
The descendants of Mr. Fletcher
Pitcairn Island.

He set off for home. Samuel would be expecting him.

You always have to have a few secrets, if not more, Joel thought. You can't keep on living if you don't.

Before, I had the secret I shared with Sonja Mattsson.

I have another one now.

Now I also have the letter to Pitcairn Island.

But he wasn't absolutely sure that he wouldn't tell the Greyhound about the letter. It was at least as important to share secrets as it was to keep them.

Perhaps she would think it was childish? Writing letters to somebody who might not even exist. On an island at the other side of the world, as far away as it was possible to get.

Too bad.

He had learnt how to kiss.

But he was still childish. And he wanted to carry on being childish.

For as long as he enjoyed being childish.

He was walking quickly because it was cold.

Just as he opened the gate, and noticed Samuel's shadow in the upstairs window, it started snowing.

I wasn't surprised this time, Joel thought.

Snow is silent. It creeps up on you.

But this time I was ready for it.

Then he dashed in through the door. Everything felt better now. It was Christmas. Samuel had bought a Christmas tree that they'd helped each other to decorate. There was a smell of candles. And the Greyhound was around, and would still be around tomorrow.

Samuel was in the kitchen, waiting for him. He looked serious. Joel was afraid Samuel would tell him off for being out so late.

"I'm on holiday," Joel said. "I don't need to get up early tomorrow."

Samuel was still looking hard at him.

"Simon is dead."

Joel heard what Samuel said. But it didn't sink in.

"No," said Joel. "Simon's not dead. I talked to the doctor. He said that Simon was getting better. He'll probably even be able to speak again."

"Simon is dead," said Samuel again.

Joel shook his head.

"He seemed to be getting better," Samuel explained, "but then he just died. Stopped breathing. And was gone."

"But why?"

Joel didn't have any other questions. That was the only one he could think of.

Why did Simon have to die, when Joel had rescued him and dragged him ashore like a shipwrecked sailor in a sea of snow?

"Death always creeps up on you and makes a mess of everything," said Samuel.

Joel felt as if he had a knot in his stomach. He thought about the dogs. Were they sitting on the steps outside Simon's front door, howling? And the hens in the cab of the truck. How were they grieving?

"Simon can't be dead," Joel said again. "I've borrowed his guitar. He can't die until I've returned it."

"Simon is dead," said Samuel yet again.

And now the message finally got through to Joel. Simon really was dead.

Later, during the night, when he couldn't sleep, Joel curled up on the window seat. He tried to make himself as small as possible, so that there was room for him. Just like there used to be.

This is evidently what life is like, he thought. Always, all the time. Death can intrude and make a mess of things at any time. So why should he insist on living to be a hundred? And going to bed in the snow in order to toughen himself up?

I have to choose, he thought. Now that Simon is dead. Decide if I'm going to carry on being childish or not. If that's a choice I have.

He tried to find an answer. But there wasn't one.
In the end, he fell asleep on the window seat.

And the snow kept on falling silently through the night.

Written in the house by the river

My name is Joel. My dad is Samuel. Our surname is Gustafson. On the wall in the house where we live is a ship called Celestine, in a display case. I think it is similar to the Bounty. We live on the bank of a river where ships never ride at anchor. All that flows past here is tree trunks, logs; the water is cold, there aren't any palm trees. But in the summer we hear the whining of mosquitoes.

We're going to travel to Pitcairn Island, my dad and I.

I can't say when we'll arrive, because I don't know when it will be possible for us to set off. Maybe when the snow has melted away and spring has come? One can always hope.

Do you ever have snow on Pitcairn Island? It's not possible to work that out by looking at a map. But if you do have snow, I can bring my skis with me. Samuel is very bad at skiing.

We've read about your mutiny, and we think you did the

246

right thing. Captain Bligh was a cruel man. He didn't understand how bad things were for the crew. How hard it can be
to leave paradise. Where women wander along the beaches in
transparent veils with nothing on underneath. Fletcher was a
hero. May he rest in peace.

We shall be traveling to Pitcairn Island in order to live
there. Do you have a B&B place? It will have to be cheap, as
we don't have much money.

Samuel wonders if there's a school. But I don't think that's
very important.

Samuel can chop down trees in the forest. He's very good
at that. If you have a forest, of course.

As for me, Joel Gustafson, I'm still very childish. But I
don't normally cause any trouble.

When we get there, it would be great if a woman wearing
transparent veils could surprise Samuel on the beach.

Me as well.

With best wishes,

Joel Gustafson

Written this 19th day of December.

ABOUT THE AUTHOR

HENNING MANKELL is the prizewinning and internationally acclaimed author of novels for both adult and young readers. His Inspector Wallander mysteries dominate bestseller lists across Europe. Born in a village in northern Sweden, Mankell divides his time between Sweden and Africa, where he works with AIDS-related charities. He is also the director of Teatro Avenida in Maputo, Mozambique. Mankell's previous novels for young people about Joel and his father are *A Bridge to the Stars* and *Shadows in the Twilight,* both available from Delacorte Press.